I'M SECRETLY AN IMPORTANT MAN

STEVEN JESSE BERNSTEIN

Foreword by Grant Alden
Edited by Jim Jones & Deran Ludd
Art Direction by Heather Werner & Alice Wheeler

Manufactured in the United States of America

ISBN 0-9638594-1-2

First Printing, First Edition, February 1996

Cover Design: Heather Werner and Alice Wheeler
Cover Photo: © 1988 Alice Wheeler
Back Cover photo (Fenimore Hotel) © 1995 Alice Wheeler
Other photographs © Alice Wheeler

Interior typefaces:
Text—Palatino
Titles and footers—Copperplate

This Book is Dedicated to Jesse: Mentor,
Inspiration, Friend and Co-Conspirator.
We Miss You.

Thanks You: Mary Jo Bunger, Jeff Bernstein, Phoebe Jewel, Jake London, Marie Norris, Hannah Parker, Bruce Pavitt and Jeff Stookey.

The Steven J. Bernstein Archive has been instrumental in the preservation and organization of Jesse's literary estate. Without the cooperation of the Archive, especially Leslie Fried, we could not have accomplished this project.

TABLE OF CONTENTS

Editors' Preface

Criteria used in selecting stories for this collection included a desire to represent the broad sweep of Jesse's short prose work and our personal favorites.

Some of these works are rawer than Jesse would have wanted them to be when published—but he is not here to oversee the project. The only editing we did was for story integrity and clarity.

Jesse often punctuated his stories as a tool when performing these pieces. Rather than standardize it we've kept most of the punctuation the way it was written. We've also retained his personalized spellings of certain words.

When Jesse wrote the copyright date on a story, or when we had reliable secondary sources, we included the dates when the stories were written.

The publication of *I am Secretly an Important Man* is a contribution to making Jesse's work more widely read and more accurately understood.

Jesse Bernstein and William S. Burroughs at the Moore Theater, Seattle 1988

Jesse Bernstein at the Scargo Hotel on First Ave., Seattle 1986

Jesse Bernstein at the Scargo Hotel on First Ave., Seattle 1986

Foreword

By Grant Alden

The facts are these: Steven J. Bernstein was born December 4, 1950 in Los Angeles, California. He died, by his own hand, early in the morning of October 22, 1991 in Neah Bay, Washington, a small Pacific Coast town on the Makah Indian Reservation.

In between, little is certain.

Steven Jay Bernstein. Not Jesse, though that's the name by which he was known as an adult. Well known he was—in Seattle, anyway—by small, tight circles of friends, many believing themselves to be his best and closest companion, often unaware even that other circles might exist. Jesse, careful always to keep those circles from touching (it's an old addict's survival skill), lest a bubble burst.

We first met for a mid-afternoon breakfast June 14, 1988. He wanted to place his career in some kind of order for a short introduction to an interview he had conducted with William Burroughs, Burroughs at last having consented to do a reading in Seattle.

Jesse began, after a gulp of coffee:

"I was born on December 4th, 1950 in Los Angeles. I didn't do well in school. I'm doing better in school now. Actually I quit school early and spent a number of years back and forth between institutions and the country at large. I am not a Viet Nam veteran. I went to the draft board wearing lady's clothes, eating a kielbasa. Claimed to be a Christian and tried to convert the people at the draft board. They threw me out. I was a professional musician for a long time. A bass player and a vocalist, and wrote a lot of songs. I've done a lot of things. I was a really good dishwasher and a really good ditch digger, those are two things I'm very proud of. I don't do either of 'em anymore. I was a drunk and a drug addict for a long time. Alternately, not both at the same time. I don't do either of them anymore. It's not very dramatic, I just lost interest. It didn't help my writing any."

Bernstein sat before the tape recorder again in the fall of 1990 on a similar errand. He wanted liner notes for what would become the *Prison* CD on Sub Pop. Originally conceived as a set of acoustic songs, recorded live before the inmates of the Special Offenders' Unit at the State Reformatory in Monroe, Washington, *Prison* evolved into a collection of poetry accompanied by Steve Fisk's sampled soundtrack. Jesse lived to hear only "No No Man" completed.

Those two interviews, augmented by the kindly shared memories of jazzman Peter Leinonen, promoter/manager Larry Reid, artist Alison Slow Loris and actress Lori Larsen, became the informal oral history which follows.

Ambiguity and false trails—they have their place, too.

And Jesse was a story-teller, first.

Steven J. Bernstein was born in Los Angeles, second son to a Russian Jewish family. The Bernsteins lived with his maternal grandfather, but midway through his fourth year Jesse contracted polio and spent a year in hospital.

"He told me some things enough different times that I began to pick out the parts that stayed the same," Alison Slow Loris says. "His parents' marriage seems to have begun falling apart nearly the same time he was born. His father's response to that was violence. For some reason—Jeff [Jesse's older brother] has told me this, too—the rage seemed to focus on Jesse.

"And then he got polio. He was not actually completely paralyzed, as he sometimes liked to say, but was very largely immobilized for the best part of a year, living entirely in his head and having really painful spinal things done to him from time to time, [treatments] that were half diagnostic and half supposed to make it better, but were extremely painful."

"My father was an inventor, a mechanical designer, a machinist," Jesse said. "My mother was, at the time, a pianist. She used to sit and practice on a big, red mahogany upright grand. I spent a lot of time underneath the piano bench when I was very small, listening to my mother playing. She could sing well, too. I actually started being involved with music instantly upon being born. It wasn't something I picked up later.

"As soon as I was old enough to sit on the piano bench I was allowed to play with the piano. I figured out a lot of things. When I was, oh, a young kid—I'm a little hard with the numbers, eight, nine, ten—I got pretty serious about trying to compose and write music. Just in my head. Later I did a certain amount of transcribing the stuff that was in my head. Then my mom wanted to get me piano lessons; I guess she felt that I showed a certain amount of talent. The piano teacher canned me after three weeks. She told my mom that I was better off left alone," he laughed. "Because I wouldn't practice anything she gave me; I kept coming in with my own stuff."

Steven also developed an active interest in science. The only concrete reminder of his childhood curiosity is a photograph from the *Evening Outlook* (presumably a Los Angeles area shoppers weekly) reproduced in Sub Pop's *Prison* press kit: "Man with plan is young Steven Bernstein, 10, of Mar Vista, who after two years' research finally developed a feasible rocket plan which he submitted to Douglas Aircraft. He discusses possibilities of constructing his rocket with Works Manager Nelson H. Shappell, as they view the Thor model."

Bright young Steven's star fell quickly. "My parents were divorced when I was six," he said. "Ultimately this little scene of growing up in a house with grandpa fell apart. My dad moved on, and grandpa had moved to a hotel in downtown Los Angeles. I just drove my mother nuts. I'd come home whenever I felt like it. I liked to hang around down by the beach and to walk through long networks of alleys, picking through trash cans. That was my trip for years. Or I'd take long walks, all the way from the beach to downtown on Venice Boulevard. I'd find myself down there late at night, poking around the magazine stands. I thought it looked very cool to smoke cigars; I don't know where I got that. I started swiping cigars. I was a little kid walking around downtown LA at night smoking these big, long brown cigars."

Loris theorizes that Jesse's mental illness corresponds to the onset of puberty. There is strong evidence that the problem was a genetic mismatch that left Bernstein's brain slightly too large for his skull. In December 1990 Jesse went to the University of Washington Medical Center in Seattle and there they ran some tests. Jesse felt there were physiological reasons for his problems. At the hospital, results from Magnetic Resonance Imaging found scarring on his frontal lobes. The physical problem was a small area that connected the two frontal lobes that would swell, pushing the frontal lobes against the skull. Loris stated, "And all these little swellings were like little seizures." Consequently, Jesse went to Harborview Medical Center and was tested for epilepsy. They monitored him for one week and found no trace of that condition. Loris added, "The doctors gave him a lot of really interesting information about what the problem was, but they didn't have any solutions. And, in fact, there was a lot of cumulative brain damage by then." Based on all of the above information Jesse decided he no longer needed anti-psychotic drugs.

"When he was having a bad time with the illness," she adds, "when he was drinking and when he wasn't drinking, his eyes were so big that they looked like they were going to just explode out of his head. There was pressure within. His whole brain was swelling. Some of the flavor of pieces he's written about his childhood, like 'The Face,' the feeling is very much from that period.

"He was just feeling crazy and not wanting to be interfered with. He started locking himself in the garage, and one time he threatened to kill [his mother] if she didn't leave him alone. She was fairly poor. She couldn't afford expensive private treatment. They had a court hearing, and committed him for his own good. They threw him into a psychiatric institution for poor people, including the criminally insane. And they threw him in with adult men. The staff was fairly perverse there, too. It was kind of a toss-up whether on any given day he was going to get raped by his fellow patients or the guards.

"I'm not sure exactly what brought his father back into this, but his father came to find him and got him out. I don't think he was there even six months, but it was more than enough. He had grown up in East LA, then he'd been in this institution. His father took him to Ventura County, and put him in a suburban school, with all the rich kids. I don't think he stuck it out even a year, it was so bizarrely unrelated to anything he'd ever known. He ran away, he went to San Francisco, he lived on the streets."

"In school I did about average, really, when you look at the whole thing stretched out," Jesse said. "The end for me was the ninth grade. I never went to school again. I don't think I could have been more disinterested, and felt more enslaved. And by that time I was very interested in playing music, and I liked to paint, too. When I got out of [that institution] I really felt alienated. I didn't really trust anybody. There was no way that I could plug into anything that anybody had mapped out for me, that I had mapped out for myself."

Bernstein arrived in San Francisco in the mid-60s. "He was never a hippie," Loris says. "It was the jazz scene, the narcotics scene, the end of the beat scene down there. And he became a whore. Paid his rent that way in one hotel with some old queen. And learned to play jazz bass, that's what he thought he was, a bass player, when he first came to Seattle. As a boy junkie on the street he would tend to wind up in some kind of jail or another from time to time. He always said he hated Christmas because there were four or five years in a row he spent Christmas in a mental institution or a prison."

"I never really returned home after the first time [in a mental hospital]," Jesse said. "I lived in various places, down in San Diego, San Francisco, North Beach, here and there." He paused, remembering. "Wound up getting myself in trouble. Narcotics. Got busted. Spent quite a bit of time getting shuffled from one jail to another. Not certain whether I was an adult or a child," he laughed, "they couldn't make up their minds what they were going to do with me, and I was very uncooperative. Did some solitary time. Eventually I escaped, which is a whole big long story, real complicated. It wasn't one of these digging a little tunnel things, or wire cutters. It took some arranging, to escape.

"I wound up in Seattle, trying to get across the state line as quickly as I could. I was trying to get to Canada, actually; I had no desire to go to Seattle at all. I was sixteen-ish, and tried to get across the Canadian border, and I didn't have any ID, and I had $5," he laughed. "[The border guards] didn't want to know anything about me, they just wanted me to go away. They got me a ride to Blaine, left me in a laundromat and I caught a bus to Seattle. And that's how I wound up here."

Peter Leinonen was virtually the first person Jesse Bernstein (Steven Jay became 'Jesse' on the lam, but the name fit, and stuck) met when he arrived in Seattle in the fall of 1966. Already a veteran musician, Leinonen had played in an early Northwest rock band and in a folk group before returning to his first love, jazz.

"There was a little cafe called the Pancake House," Leinonen begins. "Right nearby was a club called the Llahngælhyn, where I was the house bass player. The last city he'd been in was San Francisco, where he played trumpet and bass. That first night Jesse was wearing this big old raincoat. It was way, way too big for him, because he was really skinny, but he had a voice that was much older than his age, and he had a real tattered copy of *Naked Lunch,* which he handed to me the first night we met, and said, 'You gotta read this book.' I actually stayed up all night and read it.

"For the rest of the time that club existed I played there every weekend. The house band played for the customers, and basically split up tips and the door charge. We didn't make a lot of money, but we were developing as jazz artists. After one or two in the morning, when the other gigs in town shut down, the local stars would come in and play until five or six in the morning. Then, when they quit, we'd go back up and play again. We'd sleep on the floor, wake up in the middle of the morning, go to the Pancake House and eat, and the whole thing would start again the next day.

"The first great jazz mentor Jesse had was a guy named Phineas Newborn, Jr., a great jazz pianist from Memphis. He was probably the pianist who would have come after Art Tatum in jazz history, but he was crazy. He got crazier and crazier and crazier, was severely abused in mental hospitals, and eventually died. When Jesse was first put in a psychiatric hospital—this is in all of his early work—he got gang raped. We recorded 'Choking on Sixth' together, which is all about that. Well, the hospital authorities weren't equipped to get Jesse any official protection, but Phineas Newborn was in this same psychiatric hospital—it might have been Camarillo, the hospital Charlie Parker was in, I know Jesse did some time there—and he was a big guy who played the piano all day. So, to protect Jesse from the other inmates, the psychiatric hospital's staff started sticking him in the practice room where Phineas Newborn spent all his time. Jesse actually sat on that floor there and listened to that piano. I think that is where his jazz ear was developing. That's really a great time to have that kind of exposure. Jesse never became a great piano player, but he got a great ear.

"I never was in the San Francisco club he hung out in, but I got the feeling it was as much about dope as it was about playing, and that the standards of musicianship weren't high. We were playing more experimental stuff, and so Jesse found the Llahngælhyn a little intimidating. There was a whole group of people who hung around the Llahngælhyn who were junkies—that was their primary interest. Jazz clubs were great places for drug users, because they were dark, intimate, the music was great, they went all night, and it was a good place to score. The longer Jesse was in town, the more I associated him with that bunch, although he did start playing the same lounges I was playing in.

"I almost fell out of touch with Jesse, but we had a mutual friend, Heather Hammond, and Heather became Jesse's lover—that's Daemon's mom. Heather was the best singer in town. She's still playing music, she lives in Alaska now."

Peter ran into Jesse again a few years later, when Leinonen's band, Mirage, began to be billed with Bernstein's band, Juju (Jesse was back to playing trumpet). "They were psychedelic [rock] bands. And as great as they were, we were on LSD every day and so, to tell you the truth, I can't remember Jesse's songs. The only reason I can remember my own is because I wrote them down. That was a wonderful time, and I wish I had a clearer memory of it, but I'm talking about two years of being on acid continuously. During Mirage and Juju, we used acid like fuel, it fueled our work and performances."

Leinonen remembers Jesse working as a song writer after Juju disbanded. "He was writing for a travelling show called Goose Creek Symphony that went around the Northwest on a bus. There were a couple of folk-rock rock-festival acts that took Jesse on the road as a lyricist. There was a long period when he was writing for groups that were much more established than he was. They'd let him live on the bus, feed him, and buy him drugs. I think it was later that he became meticulous about his copyrights."

"I wrote a song here in Seattle that got lifted," Jesse insisted, "along with ten others. Two of those songs a friend claimed to have heard on a jukebox in the Midwest. I don't have any reason to doubt him. They apparently didn't go very far; I never heard them out here. I was living in a hotel down on First Avenue and I was getting most of my food out of the dumpsters down at the Public Market. There was nothing I could do about it, anyway. I didn't know what a copyright was." (Jesse's later fussiness about copyrights seems to have forced Sub Pop to create their first recording contract, for "Come Out Tonight" on Sub Pop *200*. When Nirvana demanded a contract shortly thereafter, Sub Pop had Bernstein's for a blueprint.)

"He didn't get good [as a jazz musician]," Leinonen says, with some frustration. "He had the talent and the ear, but he got involved with drugs before he got good....Jesse was either copping or nodding most of the time during that period. He certainly had the ear to be great, he had more talent than me. But he didn't have the discipline."

"He went to a community college, probably in the mid- to late-70s," Loris says. "Heather would drop Daemon on him and let him bring Daemon up for a year or so, and then she'd come back and swoop him away again. And Jesse was always really wonderful with children. He must have been still a junkie when he went to school, but he was trying to appear to become a stable and responsible person so that he had some sort of hope of getting custody of his kid, which was completely impossible.

"He signed up for the pre-freshman composition class they put you in if you've never finished high school. The instructor looked at his first assignment and said, 'What the hell are you doing in here? You're a writer, you don't belong in here.' 'Oh, I'm a writer?'" It may not have been quite so innocent as all that; Bernstein's resume lists his first unpublished piece of fiction as "Dionysus and the Fishwife Mali", dated 1970.

Jesse wrote the chapbook *Choking on Sixth* after his stint as lyricist; Leinonen remembers it as his first published work. "He had a girlfriend in a topless club," Leinonen recalls. "One time she asked him why he didn't publish his poems, and he said it was because he didn't have the money. She asked how much it would cost, he told her, and, the way he put it, she said, 'Wait here,' and went out into the parking lot and earned the money in an hour." *Choking on Sixth* appeared in 1978.

At some point in the '70s Bernstein began a correspondence

with William Burroughs, and travelled to New York at least once. "I know Jesse was trying to do something jazz-connected there, but the stories are real vague," Loris says. "The main thing I remember him telling me about his stay in New York was that the apartment he was subletting had a pet iguana that lived under the radiator and did rodent control. [He and Burroughs] had been corresponding for a couple of years before I met Jesse in 1979.

"Jesse had somehow developed the idea that because Burroughs was famous he must be rich. So he wrote him this long, angry, drunken letter in the middle of the night, about how, yeah, he was out there in his writing when he was younger, but now he was probably just another fat, happy, middle-class guy like the rest. Burroughs wrote back, saying, 'What the hell makes you think they pay me? Grow up, kid.'"

"Eventually," Leinonen says, "Jesse went off to see Burroughs in New York, and that was about the same time I was finishing my music degree [at the University of Washington]. Burroughs told him that he should collaborate with a musician. When Jesse came back I had a record that was getting a lot of play, and I was playing at Parnell's, the top jazz club in town. Jesse came in the club and came straight up to me, and said, 'Pete, I just met Burroughs, and he wants me to collaborate with a musician, and I want you to do it.'

"After our first rehearsal, Alison said, 'Wow, Jesse came home with wings on his feet.' And it was a really great collaboration, because Jesse had just had a bout with hepatitis, and had gone straight. He'd kicked heroin and he'd kicked alcohol and he'd started writing furiously. He was writing tons of stuff as Jesse Bernstein, he was writing under a couple of other names, he was writing for the *Northwest Passage* [Seattle radical newspaper of the '70s and '80s], he was writing plays and short stories, and novels, poems, he was just an all-night writing machine, and such a perfectionist. He didn't have a computer then. If he misspelled one word, he'd wad it up and start over.

"Jesse would come in to my studio with his new writing, and start reading. I'd nail a key and a tempo from what he was doing, and usually the first time through I'd come up with a main motive, and I'd scribble some notes on my copy of the writing, and the pieces stayed in that form. Then we did *Words and Music* together, which was originally two 30-minute radio tapes for the Pacifica Network." Bernstein and Leinonen went on to collaborate on a series of operas and a variety of other performances.

Bernstein said in 1988 that his correspondence with Burroughs began with a one-sided salvo of 81 letters in two months, inspired by *The Job*, a book of interviews with Burroughs. A small irony. Jesse didn't have many jobs. "Mostly he was on some kind of welfare," Loris says. "I don't know where he got his money when he was a junkie, and he never did, either. He said that was part of the nature of being a junkie. You have to have this much money every day to get by, and you just do it. He and a couple of his junkie friends, well, they'd break into drug stores. A lot.

"There was one pharmacy where the owner was probably a junkie himself. He was really easy-going about accepting obviously forged prescriptions. And every so often, when it was time for the Feds to come through and look at his books, count his supplies and find that things didn't match up, he'd hire a couple of people to come and do an armed robbery."

For what it's worth, no arrest records exist for Jesse (nor for Steven Jay) Bernstein amid the computers of the Washington State criminal justice system, though computerized records only go back to 1978.

"Well, he had odd jobs from time to time," Loris amends, "but they were generally fairly odd and they were real time-to-time. Mainly, the damage and the genuine inability to work a regular job for very long was so clear that, while sometimes various branches of crazy welfare would argue with each other about which one should be paying for him, there was never any argument that someone was going to have to write a check. I've always said that my generation viewed welfare as a federal arts grant."

"He knew how to live poor," Lori Lars[illegible] adds. "He was among that band from our generation who believed that [being] poor was a banner of pride, rather than something you were trying always to get out of. If we live poor, then we can do what we want, and he really lived that philosophy. His poverty got to him sometimes, but most of the time he was proud of it, and it gave him an infinite amount of freedom to be creative. And he reminded all his friends who also had leanings that way, that they could do it, too.

"He was always there at a point where you might think about having a real job. Then you'd go see Jesse and you'd make up your next job, together. When you did something of Jesse's and it worked, you really felt like you were the center of the universe. You didn't have to be in New York, you didn't have to be some other place, because you were just the coolest thing there ever was. He was able to give you that."

"I worked 16 hours a day, and so did Jesse," Leinonen says. "We always used to laugh about that. Here we are working our butts off, and everybody wants to help us, they want to give us a 'job.' For Christsake, we've got a job, we'd just like to get paid. I don't think people realize how important Jesse's job was. Just because he wasn't earning money doesn't mean he didn't have a job."

"I think all anybody really wants is intimacy with other people," Jesse said in 1988. "People want to have food to eat, some purpose for being here. Some place to sleep. Something to do. I feel like I've got some of that. I'm really fortunate in that respect. I worked on it without thinking about it, but I set it up so some of those things can't be taken away or messed with by anybody. You'd have to chop my head off to mess with it. You could take all my shit—my computer and all my crap—and blow it up or throw it out the window, and it still wouldn't stop *anything*. You'd probably get about a one-hour response out of me by doing something like that. And then I would just go find someplace else to live and get some BiC pens. Just write about that, then, about everything being gone."

Alison Slow Loris met Jesse in February of 1979. She and friends had created a *faux* cafe as an art exhibition at the Pelican Bay Cooperative, on 19th Ave. on Seattle's Capitol Hill. "Somebody dragged Jesse in, and, well, a lot of his poems were in the sort of 'green mucous and burnt flesh' style, and I wasn't too impressed," Loris chuckles. "And he was at the height of his really serious alcoholism. He stayed later and later and got more and more obnoxious, and more and more drunk. I still remember him rolling around on the floor saying, 'I just did a show, how come I can't get laid?'

"He came back the next day, somewhat more sober, and hung out with my four-year-old son, which first began to endear me to him because the kid was really being a pain. I kept running into him at odd intervals, usually early enough in the day that, although he was drinking all day, every day at that point, just to stay level, he was only actually drunk in the evenings. We left a party together in September, and in early October he came to spend the night and never left. Well, later the next day, he said, 'I don't want to leave.' I said, 'OK, well, don't leave.' And then three days later, it was 'I don't want to leave.' 'Don't leave.' A week later, he said, 'Let's get married.' 'OK.'"

Bernstein was pretty much off hard drugs by this point, and at work as a writer. "If someone had drugs and offered them to him, he would take them for old time's sake," she says. "He'd been a full-time junkie for a number of years, starting when he was probably like 16, stopping only when he was actually in prison or another institution. Probably three years before I met him, he finally got too scared of the scene for purchasing the drugs, and decided to see if he could get by on alcohol, instead."

Over the years Bernstein would periodically explore other kinds of cures. "Jesse was always in and out of born-again churches," Loris says, "He was also in and out of being a Catholic. If whatever was going on around him had some sort of spiritual aspect to it, and was really powerful, and the community was really overwhelming, he could stay off junk and alcohol for awhile. But that would never work for too many months on end."

"Alison and Jesse had just gotten married when I met him," Lori Larsen says. "He called me up out of the blue—he'd seen me in a play—and he wanted me to come to see this first attempt at a play that he was doing in a tavern in Ballard (a Seattle neighborhood). They were doing this little play called *Dead Dog*, which I then co-opted and did many, many times myself. I used to go visit him in his hotel room, up on Capitol Hill, at Jefferson on Broadway. This was right before he quit drinking. Sometimes he'd bring out his switchblade and kind of slash it around and yell with his voice and kind of scare me, and I'd run out. Jesse knew I was a gardener, so he says in that voice, 'You wanna see my mold garden?' Then he brought out these jars from under his bed, old pickles and old mustard, that he'd been growing molds on. To me that's a perfect analogy; something that was molding, he would keep around to look at and see the beauty of it."

That residential hotel on Broadway is also where Jesse's tattoos were fashioned. "That would be 1980. We quarrelled over various things...." Loris says. "He moved into the Fenimore Hotel, and eventually I wound up moving in there with him. It was full of like, gay Mexican S&M people, and strange old alcoholics who had lived there with their hot plates and their TVs for 35 years, and so on. It was a real lowlife scene. Jesse had been remembering a whole lot about his youth.

"Jesse had been the tattoo artist in a lot of the institutions he'd been in. It was a way he could get cigarettes, or protection from the bigger guys. You cannot be buried in a Jewish cemetery if you've been tattooed. That's one of the reasons that the Nazis tattooed all their concentration camp inmates, as an additional insult. Jesse had been thinking a lot about that, too. He suddenly decided that he was going to complete that identification of himself with all the poor Chicano prisoners he'd been in jail with in California [one tattoo reads "El Vato Loco"—The Crazy Dude] and all the concentration camp survivors he knew.

"He did them all at once, in a three- to six-week period. We were drinking a lot of Irish whiskey and living in this little sleazy hotel room with a big dog that was afraid of thunderstorms. Jesse couldn't see either. Jesse's eyes were very bad. They were always very bad. But he used to say that sometimes for relief from the hallucinations he saw with his glasses on and his brain not working right, he would just take off his glasses and have the simple hallucinations of not being able to see anything.

"The 'LIVE' and 'DEAD' [on his right and left knuckles] were some of the earliest tattoos. He started coming up with all sorts of symbols and putting them all over his hands. There was an 'A,' which was for me and later, when he needed to explain it to other women, he said it was for anarchy. Which works," she laughs. "He didn't do any more, later."

In the late '70s Bernstein began to read his poetry around Seattle at punk rock shows, and at the local punk art gallery (Rosco Louie and, later, Graven Image) run by Larry Reid and Tracy Rowland. "Jesse performed on an average of once a month at Rosco Louie," Reid says. "The idea of a poet performing at a punk rock club didn't exist, though it started,

I think, with Jesse. He was very provocative, and it wasn't at all uncommon for Jesse to engage members of the audience in violent discourse. In fact, it was part and parcel of his performance to engage the audience in a shouting match. Quite often performances involved death threats, and he would brandish weapons.

"The first 'poetry slam' [in Seattle] took place at Rosco Louie in 1980. That was the result of a poet who's still active in Seattle, Ron Dacron, who came to a reading at Rosco Louie. Jesse was telling one of his stories and Ron volunteered from the audience words to the effect of, 'Jesse, you're full of shit.' Jesse charged into the audience and they were chin to chin screaming at each other. About a month later, Ron was doing a reading at Blanchard Street Studios [in downtown Seattle]. Jesse interrupted his performance brandishing a gun, which turned out to be a squirt gun, but...he ended up squirting Ron in the face, and that turned into a bit of a brawl, and Jesse ended up getting thrown out.

"I decided to put the two together. I had [graphic designer] Mark Michaelson make a boxing poster, it was called 'The Battle of Heavyweight Prose.' Inside the gallery I built a boxing ring, I had a referee and a panel of three literary judges. The format was such that they would come out for three minutes and read short pieces. The referee had to separate them a couple times. Jesse won on points. There was no knockout, but I think Jesse got one round 10-8, on a knockdown. It was hilarious.

"At one of the performances I'd bought him two bottles of Thunderbird, and there was a little backstage at Rosco Louie. When something wasn't just right, he took a full bottle and just turned around, blindly drunk, and threw it up against the wall, and missed my wife, Tracy, by about an inch. We had to pick glass out of her hair. He didn't try to hit her; he didn't see her. But, then, moments later he came out and did an insanely perfect performance, and you just can't stay mad at somebody like that, you know?"

"The first time he got sober was in the summer of '81," Loris says. He stayed sober maybe six weeks after he got out [of a rural alcohol detox center]. It was really hard, because he wasn't on any sort of medication then. People, including him, just assumed the problem was alcohol, and that if he stopped drinking he could get over that. When I got to see what his illness looked like, when he'd been sober for a couple years, I think it was basically neurological. There was psychiatric stuff that got piled on top of it, because of some other things that were done to him, but the illness itself was almost a mechanical sort of electrical misfiring of the brain. All the therapy in the world is not going to deal with the physical problem. So those first few months of sobriety without any medication were just completely impossible.

"Then he started drinking again. It was November. We'd been semi-homeless for a while. He was drinking again, having a really bad attack of the illness, and he was hallucinating constantly. One day it was wigs, on every surface in the room. Where that came from, who knows, but he got to the point where if he had to look at those wigs any longer he was going to want to kill himself. We went to Harborview, and they were full. They called around for a bed in a psych ward, and sent him out to a hospital in [the Seattle suburb of] Renton.

"The first question the doctor asked him was, 'How long have you been self-medicating?' It was the first time anybody had put together the fact that he was always on something, and the fact that he had a problem. They started him on lithium, and that was what made it possible for him to live and work, with some other [psychiatric] drugs coming and going for problem times. The first thing he wrote after he was sober, and we'd settled down into a fairly quiet life-style, was the novel *Hermione*. And, without any individual details being the same, the overall atmosphere in *Hermione,* in which one person is deeply enclosed in a sickness and everybody else is reacting to that, was related to his take on how it had been in that first solid year of sobriety, when he was just kind of hanging on to himself, and everything was going crazy all around him."

Bernstein's marriage to Loris came to an end in the mid-'80s. "We were always friends," she says. "We truly, literally did stop being married to make sure we could stay friends." In the summer of 1986 he married Lori Chambers, an abstract painter, and lived for a time on a houseboat with her. Then Jesse moved into what would essentially be his last home, the Ontario Hotel (another low-end residential hotel) on Airport Way S., in a mostly industrial neighborhood he called "the gray zone." In 1987 he began his love affair with Leslie Fried, a scenic artist and muralist. They remained together until Bernstein's suicide, and Fried is now executor of his literary estate.

By then the punk rock caricature of Jesse Bernstein had become a mixed burden. He was still working as a playwright and actor, and writing librettos for Peter Leinonen (and had, much earlier, been a pupil of the painter Michael Spafford), but few in his punk public were aware of these other disciplines.

"I had an experience recently," he said in 1988, "where I read poems to a group of people who were determined to see me as being very cynical, and to see whatever I got up there to say as being very funny and very cynical. Funny in a harsh sense. What I had done was get up there to read some love poems. They were sincere: I meant them. In fact, the woman to whom they were written was right there just inside the stage lights so I could see her. And the people laughed and they laughed and they laughed, no matter what I did." Jesse was reading to Leslie Fried.

"In our culture, everything is a drug," Bernstein said. "If it's not a drug, people don't want to buy it. I can make that clearer: People want something done to them. Basically people are offering themselves to be raped. They pay to be raped. Repeatedly. By anyone who will do it to them, by anyone who's capable of doing it to them, of overpowering them, of sticking it into them. It's a drug effect. People take drugs like that. You take 'em—you stick a needle in your arm, you press the plunger, and it's got heroin in it, say, or good speed, right? It's out of control. Now. There's nothing you can do about it. It's gonna overpower you. Take it: Can you take it?"

At the end of that interview, he added this: "It's nobody's fault. I don't think people are bad for wanting sensation, wanting to feel something. I feel no sense of condemnation towards those who choose to use a lot of drugs. I find them difficult to live around, but I feel no condemnation towards them. These are hard times. If people want to be anesthetized, or they want to feel something..."

The final performance of Big Black, a legendary Chicago punk band in which Steve Albini first came to prominence, was held at the Georgetown Steamplant in south Seattle. Jesse Bernstein opened, reading from *Personal Effects*, a novel he envisioned as an advanced form of Burroughs' cut-up composition. That is, Jesse wanted to write something you could pick up anywhere, set down anywhere, start over, and have the whole piece somehow work. In readings, he would simply randomly select pages. That night he responded to a heckler, "This is music, asshole," a phrase Big Black sampled and used throughout the balance of the evening.

"As good as Big Black was at that Steamplant show," Larry Reid says, "I remember Jesse, you know? I was watching the videotape, maybe a year ago, and right in the front is a very young, well-scrubbed Kurt Cobain. During Jesse's set he's right up in the front row. He's leaning on the stage, and completely eating up Bernstein." In 1991 Bernstein opened for D.O.A. in Canada. Later that year he opened for Jello Biafra at the OK Hotel in Seattle. He also performed with Jim Carroll, Kathy Acker, and a variety of other underground and cutting-edge writers.

In the end, though, Jesse couldn't stay sober. Alison Slow Loris suggests that he returned to drugs and alcohol when he was no longer able to take lithium. "[It] destroyed his liver, and he had to stop taking it," Alison Slow Loris says. "That was probably a year and a half before he died. Narcotics were much better than either alcohol or psycho-drugs in that they didn't affect his ability to write, they didn't affect his creative process. It just chilled out the stuff that was getting in the way."

"Jesse called me from the airport," Leinonen says. "'Pete, something really horrible has happened.' I said, 'What's that?' He said, 'Well, my uncle's sick, but that's not what it is.' 'Well, what is it?' He said, 'I just bought a drink.' And he'd been on the wagon for ten years, and he knew he couldn't have one drink. I said, 'Jesse, I'll be right there, just tell me where you are. Hang on, I'll get right there.' He said, 'It's no use, I'm getting on a plane in 20 minutes, there's nothing you can do about it.' He went down [to Los Angeles], and when he came back he was a drunk again.

"The last few months of his life, every time he'd come over to see me, he'd have some groupie with him, someone who was enamored of the fact that Jesse was a Sub Pop guy. And he was liking the attention of all these kids who had moved to Seattle to be around the rock scene. Jesse was kind of an elder statesman role model, and everybody wanted to be around him. And he was not immune to vanity."

Jesse always had a story, and told it well. Perhaps he made low-budget films in California, and perhaps some were porno flicks. He had roles in two serious films, both produced in Seattle—Jesse was the best part of Robert McGinley's *Shredder Orpheus* and his co-starring role in Lynn Wegenka's *Birthright* was his major acting accomplishment. How much time he actually spent in New York City is hard to sort out. Whether he really escorted a beautiful Finnish secret agent to punk rock clubs in Seattle for a couple days, we'll never know. He told me the story twice, though. Did he seriously contemplate medical school, did he work for a time in a steel factory, as a medic at minor league hockey games, did he really use a live shotgun on a guerilla film shoot being financed by Francis Ford Coppola...does it matter?

His work mattered. Once, trying to explain heroin, he said, "Look, I fixed twice a day, nodded out for half an hour. Then I went to my job, and then I came home and wrote."

One day he didn't come home to write. He left behind three sons, Daemon Bernstein, Alexander Quinn and, as the will he signed October 9, 1991 says, "a third child whom I am not close to whose name is Harmon." He also left behind two step-sons, Daniel and Julien Fried. And a body of work.

Slim Moon and Jesse Bernstein at a show, Seattle 1990

Jesse with typewriter at Scargo Hotel, Seattle 1986

Jesse Bernstein at the Moore Theater, Seattle 1988

Come Out Tonight

FORECAST IN CHROME AND PLASTIC. TYRANTS BREATHING ALLOY OF SLAVERY, PLANET HUNGER, VERSIONS OF JACKIE O. SHERRY, SHERRY BABY, WON'T YOU COME OUT TONIGHT? AND THE STARS WHISPER LIKE OLD BLOOD AT THE EDGES OF THE BODY OF NIGHT. SHE STOOD WITH ONE HAND ON THE PHONE FOR FOUR HOURS, POISED AS THOUGH ONLY A FEW SECONDS HAD PASSED. I WATCHED HER THROUGH THE CRACK BETWEEN THE SHADE AND THE SILL. SHE WAITED FOR A FORECAST IN HUMAN TREMBLING, TOGETHER WITH OTHER IMPORTANT WOMEN. COME, COME, COME OUT TONIGHT. THE WORLD SUFFERS FOR HER: THE CLOCK HURRIES LIKE A TERRIFIED ANIMAL, THEN STOPS, DRIBBLING SALIVA. SHE HAS EATEN CHICKEN PIE AND BUBBLEGUM. FOR A MONTH THE LUFTWAFFE LIVED ON RAISINS. SAME WITH THE FRENCH, AFTER THE WAR. JACKIE O RECEIVED FRESH ORANGES FROM JOHN KENNEDY. SILLY GIRL. SHE CANNOT PUT DOWN THE TELEPHONE RECEIVER. SHE IS WAITING TO RECEIVE MY BODY OF WORK. SHE WANTS TO TAKE IT IN HER EAR. A MOTTLED FLUSH BUILDS UNDER HER CHEEKS. SHE EATS XMAS CANDY WHILE SHE WAITS. THE TELEPHONE RINGS AND RINGS. I AM NOT AT HOME. I AM WITH JACKIE O. WE ARE EATING ORANGES FROM THE PRESIDENT. WE ARE ALONE ON THE ROOF OF A PARK AVENUE PENTHOUSE. PICTURE OF MARILYN MONROE IN MY BACK POCKET MOLDED BY HEAT AND SWEAT TO THE SHAPE OF MY BUTTOCKS. YOU ARE GRIPPING THE PHONE SMILING, EATING CANDY, CRYING. I AM WITH THE IMPORTANT WOMEN, NOW. I AM SECRETLY AN

IMPORTANT MAN. HANG UP THE PHONE. I CAN'T DANCE WITH YOU ANYMORE. GO TO YOUR FREEZER AND GET A POPSICLE. GO TO YOUR TV. TURN ON YOUR TV. YOU WILL SEE ME AND JACKIE O. SHE WILL BE TAKING IT IN THE EAR, MY BODY OF WORK. IN THE PLANETARIUM. YOU WILL RECEIVE A FORECAST. I WILL ALWAYS BE MORE IMPORTANT THAN YOU. YOU WILL NEVER BE IMPORTANT ENOUGH. YOU WILL NEVER BE ON THE WHIP-HAND END OF SLAVERY, NEVER BE THE ONE TO WIELD HUNGER AGAINST HUMANITY. HEAVEN WILL NEVER BE AN EXTENSION OF YOUR BODY. YOUR BODY WILL ALWAYS BELONG TO SOMEONE ELSE. THE PICTURE OF MARILYN MONROE FLUTTERS ACROSS THE ROOF, STEAMING, SHAPED LIKE ME. SHAPED LIKE MY ASS. THE SKY IS FILLED WITH ORANGES DURING THE WAR. WE EAT THEM. THE PRESIDENT IS ALONE IN A ROOM. HE IS UNIMPORTANT. AS WE EAT HIS ORANGES THE SKY GROWS BLACKER. THE MOON RIPENS AND TURNS RED. IT ROTS AND IS SWALLOWED BY THE DARKNESS. YOU ARE STILL BY THE PHONE. IT IS RINGING AND RINGING, DEAD. SHERRY, SHERRY BABY, WON'T YOU COME OUT TONIGHT? IT IS COMPLETELY DARK. THE EARTH FREEZES. YOU PUT DOWN THE RECEIVER AND GO TO THE WINDOW. COME, COME, COME OUT TONIGHT.

1989

Big Man with Tatoos

It is a trick I learned as a kid. You jack off your throat like this and then spit. Everyone—especially the girls—gets disgusted.

You see all these people? They're all watching me. They're looking at my tattoos, watching my face turn purple as I squeeze my throat tighter and tighter. I don't mind being looked at.

I like it.

The guy on the ground is my partner. Don't mess with him. He is not a friendly sort of dude. If you want to know what ugly is, ask him. But he is a good guy, too.

We drove up here from Santa Monica two days ago. We were going to Canada, but my car broke down in Renton. We just got on a bus and here we are. A couple of fucking losers, I guess.

Anyway You Cut Me

At 15 I was a good piece, any way you cut me up. The old men would gulp back their spit, swooning quietly behind dark glasses. But I always spotted the sheen of sweat on their slick, purple noses. And the tired vapors of their bodies rising from their hair and eyebrows. An oily yellow halo swam like a half-invisible ribbon round the tables of such men. I often wept with pity while fucking them. Of course they mistook this for passion. And I suppose it was passion, of a sort.

"I'm not really queer, you know, but you're pretty cute, and I know you need the money. I'd just like to help you out. You're a writer? Isn't that what you said? Well I'm drunk, so what the hell? What the hell?"

At this point I always felt like killing them, knocking them over the head with a sap or a pipe, knifing or shooting them as soon as we were out the door. Instead I said: "Me neither. I'm not queer either, really. You're right: It's the money. *I may be young, but I'm very talented."*

And we'd leave, like two old buddies. Buy a bottle and head up to my room. I paid the rent on the room with that lost, lean body, too. Two old buddies: me and the landlord, me and every high-blood-pressure fatso on Broadway. And there were so many of them...so many old buddies on the street, when I was a kid.

I wept, the different flavors of pity rolling down my face, licking the tears like green and pink and brown and white ice-cream off my lips. But I always ate my dessert silently, alone. I shared this childhood pleasure with no-one.

I grinned as though I was a hard, youthful man, not a boy. Those fatsos always believed me, dove into my charade headlong...by choice, of course. Come daylight they were shrewd as wasps, as hungry cats. When it came to business. Their business. But at night they were pussycats, fading moths. My business. My day.

"You want a blowjob? You want to suck me off? You want me to fuck you in the ass? *What do you want?* You put a fifty up there, on the nightstand, by the lamp, under the ashtray, and I'll do what you want. I'll give you what you want. It's a cold fifty." It was hard to lay it out in those terms, always. That was the hardest part.

Different flavors of piss: Feeling, if you like. But hunger played the greatest part in it. There were certain things I had to think of, to handle, day to day. They were just trying to help me out, of course, those old men. Fatsos. So I'd suck 'em off or crap on their bellies or fuck 'em good, as they wished. With feeling.

Abundance. On both sides. A couple of sissies, closing a deal.

But I felt, so often, like a pink sausage. A bunch of old Germans squabbling over my taut, clear young skin. Fat clockmakers. My ass in pawn. My balls lost in pawn, up there with a little tag on them. Half-price. A cheap little prince. Cheap, small. The big-boys with their filmy teeth, all crooked. Yeah, a little weiner. Ha ha! Teensie-weensie!

Any way you cut me up: bursting, juicy! I was an expensive little boy! Mmmmm. A hot dog. Sweet meat. Relish. Mustard. Onions. Gobble-gobble. A treat. Special. A good piece. Anyway, a fifty-dollar piece.

Now I'm 29 and married and have several teeth missing and the veins on my cock are blue and my ass is very sensitive. The icy tips of my toes and fingers may have something to do with my past. But my wife says I'm a very feeling man.

I'm still good meat.

1980

How I Met My Present Wife

(Unabridged Version)

I'm going to tell you straight out: I want to fuck Richard Nixon's dead corpse. I say "dead corpse" because what we have right now, you know—the retired gentleman in San Clemente—is already a corpse...a living corpse. And, of course, I don't want to fuck that, at all. No, I have turned it over in my mind a lot and alive there is nothing sensuous whatsoever about Nixon. It is the dead thing I want. And, yet, it is only a very subtle difference I am talking about. When his crabby and deceitful old heart gives out or cancer devours him, or a well placed sniper's bullet catches him getting out of a car—whatever it is—the effect that death has on Nixon, the transformation that happens is going to be slight, hardly noticeable. He is not much different now than he will be dead. But, there will be one critical difference: his attitude will change. And, a person's attitude is a lot of what makes them sexy, or not sexy, we all know that. Right now he is a sneaky, grasping, stingy little man. Imagine the unbearably tight, abrasive asshole on a man like that! But, when he's dead...well, he's going to relax a lot, I'm just certain of it. Old Dick's gonna finally let his hair down...open up a little, so to speak. On the other side of life, the boy will become an agreeable and very vulnerable kind of guy. Now, doesn't that make all the difference in the world? In a way that one ordinarily associates with oriental mysticism or geology, Nixon will become, I believe, somewhat graceful—Pale and slow-moving like an exotic and nearly extinct eel; lonely and soft.

This thought: the thought of R.M.N. naked and dead and alone on a bare floor (a week or two or three weeks dead, reeking of internal putrefaction, swollen with strange black and purple blotches, eyes sunken and blank) with his asshole turned up, the cheeks naturally spread by the processes of constriction and decay, the hole black and deep and gritty like a beat up steel funnel, fat, cold back twisted and un-lifelike, arms screwed out like curious hanks of meat in a broken Jesus pose, head flat and gray on its side, pressed to the floor, mouth open in a lusterless beige-pink kiss, legs bent heavily, unconscious of themselves, even in death the fingers are crossed—but, the man is utterly harmless, and shines, thusly (considering the sort of man I am talking about) with the first-and-only-ever sweetness of his existence. The brief, un-self-conscious existence of a corpse vanishing back into the omni-voracious elements. This sort of thing touches me, I'm telling you; this small, but so significant change in a man with previously no redeeming qualities, whatsoever, that I know of. Truly, the dead corpse of Nixon makes me hot; it makes my dick hard; my hips jerk and pump, reflexively. "Oh, Dick, I want you, I want you dead!" When I think of it, when I picture, you know, the act of fucking Nixon, dead....I have jacked off thinking about that—jacked off and come, and got hard again, instantly, and jacked off again. Wet, swallowing, trying to get my breath. It is a very stimulating thought, old Tricky Dicky's Dead Ass.

I'd lick the hole first, ream it out good, my tongue working and working around his shitty little butt; then, I'd spread the warm spit around, push it up in there with my finger. Look at it: a clean, eager old cornhole. Aftertaste in my mouth like rancid vanilla. Pull down my pants and drawers, down to my ankles, standing, partly naked, fine shiver like feathers on a window sill, from anticipation and bright, bestial hunger, my cock up, all the way hard, red and tightly swollen. I'd just look...stand there looking at the president, passionately, teasing myself along, doing it over and over in my mind. Out of control, I'd drop to my knees, press myself right up against the chilly corpse, my prick now painfully engorged, the blood hammering all the way up in my guts...and I'd slide it in, an inch at a time, weeping a little. "Is that okay, Dick? Does it feel good? Tell me, honey, if it hurts." Dead Dick, apparently in a state of silent and un-knowable ecstasy, doesn't say anything. I jam it in, right up to the stump, as hard as I fucking can. There is nothing up there; just cold water and rank, sticky vapor. A long, horrible, bubbling fart comes out slow, splattering my balls and belly, the hair and skin, with cold, soupy deathshit. Pat Nixon, the widow, bearing her terrible grief with remarkable equanimity, is sitting on a folding chair at a polite distance, watching and playing with herself. She giggles, whines ecstatically, then sighs a long, satisfied sigh. The Blessed Virgin of San Clemente (who first appeared in the Nixon bathroom, in 1969) has been standing nearby, silent and completely still, glowing blue and pestiferously sacrosanct; she raises her arms smartly to heaven, a definite and immediate answer to the slobbering fart from the dead-asshole's-office-of-the-high-head...dead-asshole-of-the-high-head-office...head-office-of-the-dead-high-asshole...high-office-of-the-asshole's-dead-head....Dead Dick's smoldering caboose. Who knows what she is thinking, the little Virgin...or what she is doing with her hands? Doing in her un-penetrated soul. Her brutally clean light shines on my depraved flesh, a munificent, but certain condemnation—like the singsong death sentence of a pleasant, soft-spoken gestapo executioner. Mr. Nixon is as innocent as the Blessed Virgin, herself. Only I am guilty.

The way Pat responds to the old deadman's fart....This is how it was with them, I can tell: She'd get on top and grind on his limp dick, he'd fart, and that would get her off. As for him, the fart was it—his asshole, that's where the real business was, with Richard. She could hear him moaning, tremulously, now, in the pitch of a death-silent orgasm. I didn't hear it, the little Virgin (who knows what she heard?) didn't seem to hear it, but Pat leaned back in her chair, almost falling over backwards, with her eyes closed tight, listening. So, that's what this big fart was all about.

Yes, a cadaver, cutting loose with a cold, bubbling fart, and I've got my cock stuck in it, and I'm heated up and panting...I feel myself starting to come, and then...the thing blows out a big, loud, long wet one, all over me, and my stomach and my nuts—the hair and skin—are cold and gummy...and there is the little blue Virgin, and a late-middle-aged widow sitting on a card table chair jacking herself off...and, they are watching me...and watching me...and when the body farts I can see it is important. Something meaningful is happening, here, in this cold, deserted gymnasium, under the hard, peering lights—It is not just a corpse giving off dead gas.

But, I am trying to get off, here, my fingers dug into his slack, pasty tits. Fuck his greasy little fart. "Does it feel good, Mr. President, does it feel good?" My hips pumping wildly, toes sliding back and forth on the varnished floor.

It took a lot of muscle, just keeping the body in place...holding it up so I could fuck it. Hissing noises came from Nixon's dark mouth—a kind of soft, uneven snoring. My thighs were like tight, steel springs. I was shaking with ruthless and infantile greed and impatience—the moment just before the spasm of pure, illuminated rapture we all crave.

In and out, again and again...the whole length, from knob to stump. My prick was raw from scraping against all that brittle, dead flesh...but it was okay. It was one of those times when the pain was part of getting what I wanted, was bright with promise. One doesn't complain, or look for relief. No, I fucked with terrible enthusiasm.

Dick's body shook and swayed, and his insides sloshed around and rattled against each other as I sawed away.

I couldn't come. It went on for an hour...two hours...two-and-a-half—working my way right up to the lip of the pot, but not getting the beans. I was so tired and sore, I could barely keep going. My face was buried in Nixon's wet, clay-like back. I kissed his hard, purple spine. "Dick, oh, Dick, give me satisfaction...please...please!"

The Blessed Virgin of San Clemente, gliding on sanctified feet, came over and knelt beside me. She cupped her tiny pink and blue hands around my swollen balls. My genitals rang and flushed with a truly beatific thrill. She leaned over and kissed and licked the place where my cock and Richard's asshole were joined. The pleasant mercy of this petite and luminous Saint of Heaven—mercy even for the suffering of frustrated turpitude! She earns my fervent, lifelong devotion.

Pat squats at the other end of the body, black skirt hiked up around her waist, panties down around one ankle, her cunt pressed against the former president's nose and mouth and eyes, hips gyrating out of control. Dick's face is all smeared with Pat's cunt juice...is sloppy and stinking. His head flops back and forth, listlessly.

Yes, a little difference in attitude, Dick. You're a much nicer, much sexier guy in death, half-rotted, than you ever were alive—doing that pretense of being alive. A counterfeit, a sham—you were a deadman, a corpse, all along. Dying is the most honest thing you ever did.

I came, howling, into his fetid guts, then laid there limp, my sweat cooling; I gasped hoarsely. Pat collapsed, panting, onto the president's sticky cadaver. We lay there, looking into each other's faces, engulfed in the vapors of passion, and of the putrid chemistry of decomposition. We kissed, timidly, at first—then, a long, deep, hungry kiss. I pulled her closer and worked one hand under her blouse, while I caressed her tired clitoris with the other. Pat wrapped her fingers around my cock and massaged it gently. "It's so strange, Pat, the way these things happen."

"But, wait, it was Dick I was hot for, Dead Dick, not his neurotic old lady...but maybe...maybe this is what it was all about. Maybe the president was trying to bring us together." I could feel his bones sliding around under me.

Suddenly the Blessed Virgin of San Clemente stood over us, making unknown signs of benediction. "You are married, now, you can fuck."

I looked at Pat—looked her up and down, looked her in the face. "What the hell," I thought, and rolled on top of her. My prick was hard and burning, like cherry red stone. My balls throbbed with the pulse of destiny. I slid it in slow, as though the dark head of my cock—with its one eye—were looking for the end of the universe, in there.

Dick swayed and heaved under us like a spongy old scow. "You know how it is, Dick. You couldn't expect her to give it up, forever," I murmured in his gray ear. Then, I went back to fucking my wife.

The virgin left quietly by a side door.

1986

The In Out

THIS IS NOT TV. I AM NOT ON TV. I AM IN HERE, YOU'RE OUT THERE. HERE IS THE GLASS. THAT IS WHAT SEPARATES US: THE GLASS. I CAN SEE YOU JUST FINE. I CAN SEE YOU AND YOU CAN SEE ME. THIS IS A LIVE SHOW. THERE ARE MORE PEOPLE OUT THERE THAN THERE ARE IN HERE—ALL KINDS OF PEOPLE. IT IS A VERY EXCITING SHOW, A CIRCUS OUT THERE. IN HERE IT IS ONE MAN, A MAN WITH A MICROPHONE. I AM DOING MY JOB IN HERE. MY JOB IS TO STAY ON THIS SIDE OF THE GLASS AND TALK INTO THE MICROPHONE. YOU ALL HAVE DIFFERENT JOBS. SOME PEOPLE HAVE THE JOB OF JUST STANDING AROUND. OTHER PEOPLE HURRY FROM ONE PLACE TO ANOTHER—THAT IS THEIR JOB. IF YOU WERE EATING A COOKIE, I WOULD SAY THAT YOUR JOB WAS TO EAT THAT COOKIE. SO, I AM VERY GLAD TO SEE THAT YOU ARE ALL DOING YOUR JOBS, AND DOING THEM WELL. THAT'S HOW IT LOOKS ON THIS SIDE OF THE GLASS. IT IS A BIG SHOW OUT THERE. YOU ARE PUTTING ON A BIG SHOW FOR ME. IT IS PART OF MY JOB TO KEEP TALKING THE WHOLE TIME I AM WATCHING YOU; BUT I CAN SEE YOU, I AM PAYING ATTENTION, YOU ARE ALL VERY INTERESTING, AND VERY GOOD AT WHAT YOU ARE DOING. NO-ONE CAN DO WHAT YOU DO BETTER THAN YOU ARE DOING IT, RIGHT NOW. OF COURSE, NONE OF US ENTIRELY BELIEVES THAT, NOT WHEN WE THINK THE ATTENTION IS ON US. WE BECOME CRITICAL AND SELF-CONSCIOUS, OUR FEET FEEL BIG AND HEAVY, OUR VOICES SOUND FOOLISH AND OUR HANDS DON'T KNOW WHERE TO GO—THEY HIDE NERVOUSLY IN OUR POCKETS. STILL, WE GO ON, PLODDING ACROSS THE STAGE, WAITING FOR THE CURTAIN TO FALL.

IT IS THE SAME, NO MATTER WHICH SIDE OF THE GLASS YOU ARE ON.

IT'S LUNCH TIME. WHAT IF YOU WENT INTO A CROWDED RESTAURANT, SAT DOWN, ORDERED A SANDWICH AND COFFEE, AND WHILE YOU WERE WAITING TO BE SERVED THE OTHER PEOPLE IN THE RESTAURANT—THE CUSTOMERS, WAITRESSES, EVERYONE—REARRANGED THE TABLES AND CHAIRS SO THEY COULD WATCH YOU EAT YOUR LUNCH. NO-ONE ELSE IS EATING, THEY ARE JUST WATCHING YOU, WAITING FOR YOU TO TAKE THE FIRST BITE, LOOKING AT HOW YOU LICK THE COFFEE OFF YOUR UPPER LIP, WAITING TO SEE IF ANY OF THE LETTUCE FALLS ON YOUR SHIRT. THE NEXT DAY YOU TRY ANOTHER RESTAURANT, BUT IT IS THE SAME THING. LUNCH BECOMES AN ORDEAL.YOU START CHARGING ADMISSION. PEOPLE COME FROM ALL OVER TO SEE YOU CONSUME SANDWICHES, A CHEF'S SALAD, ICE WATER, CRACKERS. AN AGENT OFFERS TO REPRESENT YOU, NATIONALLY. EATING LUNCH BECOMES A GOLD MINE. AND, AFTER A FEW YEARS ON THE ROAD, IT'S AS EASY AND NATURAL AS GETTING UP IN THE MORNING AND BRUSHING YOUR TEETH. UNTIL ONE DAY YOU GO IN THE BATHROOM RUBBING YOUR EYES, TURN ON THE WATER AND SUDDENLY YOU NOTICE THERE ARE 400 PEOPLE SITTING ON BLEACHERS, STARING AT YOU, FROM THE OTHER SIDE OF THE MIRROR. ALL YOU CAN THINK OF NOW IS LUNCH. YOU JUST GOT OUT OF BED, AND YOU'RE ALREADY THINKING ABOUT LUNCH. ON THE SECOND REFILL YOU NOTICE THERE'S NO-ONE LOOKING AT YOU. THE PERSPIRATION EVAPORATES AND YOU WALK DRY AND COLLECTED TO THE REGISTER. AFTER DOING YOUR JOB OF EATING LUNCH, YOU RETURN TO THE OTHER JOB, THE MAYBE DRAB, BUT FAMILIAR JOB, WITH A SENSE OF RELIEF.

ACTUALLY, I ONCE ATE A WHOLE BOX OF BREAKFAST CEREAL ON STAGE—LITTLE BRIGHT COLORED BALLS THAT DIDN'T WEIGH ANYTHING—IN LESS THAN THREE MINUTES. THEN I SHAVED, DID CALISTHENICS, CHECKED MY BLOOD PRESSURE, PULSE, RESPIRATION, TEMPERATURE, SAT DOWN AT A SMALL DESK WITH A TYPEWRITER AND WROTE A STORY. I DID THAT IN FRONT OF AN AUDIENCE. IT WAS MY JOB TO DO THAT, AT THE TIME. AND IT PAID.

NOW, THERE IS A STICKY POINT. EVERYONE DOES THEIR JOB, WHETHER THEY LIKE IT OR NOT, BUT SOME PEOPLE ARE

PAID AND PAID WELL, SOME MAKE JUST ENOUGH TO STAY ALIVE, AND OTHER PEOPLE ARE NOT PAID AT ALL FOR WHAT THEY DO. I, FOR INSTANCE, AM PAID TO SIT BEHIND THIS WINDOW TALKING. IT IS, IN FACT, MY JOB. I DOUBT THAT MANY OF YOU ARE PAID TO STAND ON THE SIDEWALK, ON THE OTHER SIDE OF THE GLASS, LISTENING—WHICH IS, AT THIS MOMENT, YOUR JOB. SO, THINGS ARE NOT FAIR, NO. EVERYONE DOES NOT GET A GOOD DEAL. I GOT A PRETTY GOOD DEAL: I'VE BEEN WRITING, AND STANDING IN FRONT OF PEOPLE TALKING, FOR 20 OR SO YEARS; IN THE LAST FEW YEARS I'VE BEEN GETTING PAID FOR IT.

I AM OF THE OPINION THAT EVERYONE SHOULD GET PAID, AUTOMATICALLY, FOR DOING THEIR JOB, WHATEVER IT MAY BE. WHEN YOU GO TO THE MOVIES THEY SHOULD GIVE YOU A FAT CHECK AT THE TICKET WINDOW, "THANK YOU VERY MUCH FOR WAITING IN LINE. NEXT PLEASE." WAITING IN LINE IS HARD WORK, EVERYONE KNOWS THAT. BUT, NOT ONLY DO WE SPEND A LOT OF OUR LIVES WAITING IN LINE, MOST OF THE TIME WE HAVE TO PAY TO DO IT. SOMEHOW, I FEEL THAT THAT'S BACKWARDS. ACTUALLY, EVERYTHING SHOULD BE ON A CASH BASIS, NO CHECKS OR PLASTIC. SOMEONE SHOULD BE WALKING UP TO YOU, RIGHT NOW, HANDING YOU A HUNDRED DOLLARS—TWO HUNDRED—"THANK YOU FOR STANDING HERE ON THE SIDEWALK, LISTENING TO THIS GUY TALK. YOU ARE DOING A GOOD JOB. KEEP IT UP." AND SO ON. SOME OF YOU GET PAID FOR LEAVING YOUR HOME IN THE MORNING, GOING OFF TO DO WHO-KNOWS-WHAT, BUT WHO GETS PAID FOR COMING BACK, IN THE EVENING? OF COURSE, THAT IS THE PART YOU LIKE, THE PART YOU WAIT FOR ALL DAY, BUT WHO SAYS YOU SHOULDN'T GET PAID FOR DOING SOMETHING YOU LIKE? I THINK THERE SHOULD BE A BUNDLE OF CASH WAITING FOR YOU EVERYDAY, ON THE KITCHEN COUNTER. "THANKS FOR COMING HOME."

THE WORLD IS LOPSIDED. MOST PEOPLE ARE REWARDED FOR THE WRONG THINGS. WE GET PAID FOR TORMENTING OURSELVES, FOR DOING ALL SORTS OF THINGS THAT WE WOULD RATHER NOT BE DOING."DO WHAT YOU WANT TO DO AND GET PAID FOR IT," THAT'S MY MOTTO. AND, IF YOU HAVE TO DO ANYTHING YOU DON'T WANT TO DO, GET PAID DOUBLE. IN CASH.

AM I THE PRESIDENT, YET?

NO, MY JOB IS JUST TO STAY ON THIS SIDE OF THE GLASS AND TALK. IF EVERYBODY JUST WALKED AWAY AND IGNORED ME I WOULD JUST KEEP TALKING, EMBARRASSING AS THAT MIGHT BE. IF I WAS THE PRESIDENT, I WOULD MAKE YOU LISTEN. YOU WOULD LISTEN TO EVERY WORD, AND YOU WOULD WORRY. I COULD GIVE YOU A STOMACH ACHE. IF I WAS PRESIDENT THIS WOULD BE TV. THE PRESIDENT WOULDN'T STAND IN A STORE WINDOW TALKING. MAYBE IF I WAS PRESIDENT, HE WOULD. AND, I WOULD PRINT UP LOTS AND LOTS OF MONEY—HUGE TRUCKLOADS OF IT—MOSTLY LARGE DENOMINATION BILLS. THE TRUCKS WOULD DRIVE AROUND AND MAKE SURE EVERYONE IN AMERICA GOT PAID FOR WHATEVER THEY WERE DOING. MOST OF US WOULD HAVE SEVERAL HUNDRED DOLLARS IN OUR POCKETS, AT ANY GIVEN TIME. EVEN ME. YOU, TOO.

THINK ABOUT THAT. THINK ABOUT ALL THE DIFFERENT JOBS YOU DO, EVERY DAY. YOU ARE ALL UNDERPAID. EVEN THE RICH PEOPLE ARE UNDERPAID. EVERYONE SHOULD HAVE AS MUCH OF EVERYTHING AS THEY WANT, ALL THE TIME. OH WELL.

LUNCH HOUR IS GOING TO BE OVER *SOON*. WE ALL KNOW IT. WE CAN ALL FEEL IT TICKING AWAY. WHEN IT'S ALL OVER I'M GOING TO GET OUT OF THIS WINDOW, GO SOMEPLACE AND GET A CUP OF COFFEE. THEN, MAYBE I'LL GO HOME, EAT SOME BREAKFAST CEREAL—BREAKFAST CEREAL IS MY FAVORITE FOOD—AND WRITE SOMETHING. NO-ONE WILL BE WATCHING. MY CAT WATCHES, ON AND OFF, BUT HE HAS A LOT OF OTHER THINGS TO DO BESIDES WATCH ME MUTTER OVER THE TYPEWRITER. EVEN IF I WAS ON TV, I DON'T THINK HE WOULD PAY MUCH ATTENTION; IT'S NOT HIS JOB TO WATCH TV.

1988

Of Modern Cannibals

Here I am in the street looking for a flickering orange light behind a pane of smoked glass...somewhere set into a brick wall. There is a tribe of modern cannibals. I want to see history in the making: The sharp, deadly angles and points of its jagged circumference. I want to see the extremes of each moment of future history—like watching a spreading pool of ink.

It's a dark, dark night smelling strongly of rain—that mysterious grey/brown smell. Every street name and number, every bit of trash on the street, has a hoary significance. I'm having difficulty reaching my destination, among so many symbols; the realities they cover up appear only as pale obscurities. But I know that somewhere in these streets humanity is being eaten. I'm looking for the secret meeting, wearing an armband made of braided strips of human hide; it's supposed to help me find *my* way.

I notice there is no-one else out on these streets, on this night, in this rain, this hissing rain. I follow various spiraling paths and stairways, I never encounter another soul. But I do cross paths with some of the walking dead—those who've had their middles eaten out. This loneliness is a sorry thing...a sorry state. Because of all the possible meanings of things, I'm stymied. I know how this night will end: With me stumbling, rickety legged into the first light of the sun, yelling, "This is meaningless! This is meaningless! This is meaningless!"

But, then it's possible...I might find my cannibals, after all. Eating the eyes of their prey like gumdrops. There I'll be, making tape recordings and taking photographs, laughing and snapping wishbones with the natives.

They seem to've grown up out of the bricks. That's according to *their* history. Like the old Zulus, they eat the strengths of their enemies. Power lives on; it changes hands like a baton in a relay race. As soon as one has carried it on to the next runner, they are sucked back into the earth.

Standing on the sidewalk beneath a freeway overpass, I see a blackened window and dim candle light behind it. This is set into a brick and stucco wall. It seems a strange place for cannibals to set up camp. A tame neighborhood setting. They sing loudly before and after their meal—it's a ceremonial act. I think of the simple religions of insects. These people are near the center of the city. A lot of people know what they are doing and are frightened. But, times have changed; there're no laws governing the movements of death among the human population. People learn to take their lumps. Some of them will be eaten—not the old and feeble, either. It's the young and strong and wise they're after.

I'm going down there. I check my armband. Having left the sidewalk, I am skidding down a hill, through the brambles and the mud, down toward a row of houses. I'm starting to realize that what I'm doing is dangerous, that it involves risking my life in a situation where genuine blood-lust has the run of things. In a shoulder bag are my camera and tape recorder. I maintain an archive. I do it for my own satisfaction, but I do intend to someday pass it on. My socks are getting torn by the thorns. My hands are bleeding.

I'm wondering if these people have the same response to the smell of blood as sharks. At the bottom of the hill I stop to examine my tools. Everything's in order. Here I am, playing the anthropologist...in my own city...looking for a secret society. And we aren't working at cross-purposes, either; I really think they want to be formally discovered, to be given a sheen of respectability. The cannibals want to appear in magazines and on television. Though undependable, the media continues to function. But, everything's in a state of flux. Everything. I explored a large portion of the city on foot and in the dark. I could've wound up anywhere...I could've wound up dead or half-eaten by now. My own career is a tenuous thing...my career as an archivist gathering artifacts from the present, just as it slips away behind me. It's a shaky occupation. And, of course there's no telling when I'll run out of materials...when something will fall apart and start misfiring.

You know, it's all salvage. Things like that just aren't being made anymore.

Now, I am directly across from the house. There's no point trying to peer in through the windows; they're all coated with carbon on the inside. Only a dense flickering glow, an orange glow, can be seen from the outside. So, I am listening for clues before I mount the porch steps and ring the bell. I don't hear singing—it's silent in there. They have their faces stuffed with some poor loser's ass.

So, here I am at the door. I am standing here very quietly, trying to get my courage up. I suddenly realize that even with my arm-band I am doing a very crazy thing, trying to approach the cannibals during a ceremonial meal. But this is precisely the moment I'm interested in. I just hope that somehow I can remain aloof and exempt. Everyone's dream!

I am knocking. The door is opened by an elderly gentleman. He looks like a druggist. Looking past him I see that the orange glow one sees in the windows, from the outside of the house, is not the glow of candles: A great stone firepit is built into the center of the livingroom floor. Hunks of human flesh are tied onto a spit, turning slowly over the fire. I tell the druggist who I am and why I am there. He lets me in, but he insists on taking charge of my shoulder-bag. I find a place up against a wall and hunker down. There're two cannibals squatting next to me, gnawing away at chunks of meat. They know I'm an outsider, but they're not disturbed by my presence. I feel naked without my camera and recorder. My memory isn't enough—I don't trust it. All the same, I'm working hard to remember as much as possible. No-one has said anything about what is to become of my bag, my equipment. I just have to trust the situation, trust my own senses. The old druggist is tossing wood into the firepit and singing in a low, humble voice. Actually, there is a great reverence shown the sacrifice; that's why they're being eaten...because they're worthy of reverence. The druggist is satisfied with the blaze. He steps into a small room and returns with my bag. He walks in my direction, but when he gets to me, he walks right past me. It's maddening. What is he going to do with my equipment? He stops at the end of the livingroom and stares at the flat black coating on the inside of the window. His nose is almost touching the glass. Then he turns around and starts walking back in my direction. This time when he gets to me he turns so he's facing me and formally, stiffly bows and hands me the bag. Then he cracks a broad smile. I'm starting to get paranoid. I'm thinking that maybe I'm going to be eaten. No, it would be too abrupt. It's a religious thing with these people. I've studied up on them. They don't eat people casually, just because they're there, etc. I look around. The old man is sticking close. "Is it okay if I take a few pictures and interview some of your people?" He nods that that is fine. The first photo is a beaut: Three young black men wearing brilliant yellow nylon shorts. They turn out to be triplicates and indeed, they look almost identical, right down to the same gold tooth. So, I take their picture—I take several pictures of them—and the four of us sit down cross-legged on the floor, next to the firepit. I've switched on the tape recorder.

The young triplicates are from a small country on the South American continent. The government of that country had puffed itself up and then collapsed so many times that no-one knew who was running the country, anymore. Very much like what is happening on a larger scale in the United States. They fled from their native country when they were quite young. They took up with a group of cannibals in San Bernadino, California. At that time there was still a little government left and cannibalism was illegal. They lived in the abandoned skeleton of a house. It took the triplicates quite awhile to learn English. Now they speak with exotic, musical accents.

The room has the atmosphere of a health spa, except for the stifling smoke of the fire, and the stench of burning fat and hair. But the shape of the room and the way people are hanging around the fire; it looks like they are lounging around an indoor swimming pool.

Interestingly, cannibalism did not appear as a cult in the U.S. because of the food shortage. It was always a religious thing. The early cannibals ate most of the movie stars and famous rock and roll musicians. Finally, people were afraid to enter those professions. There are still a few people left in TV. On the walls of this particular temple are bones of various powerful people. Some of the cannibals wear bits of vertebrae or toe or finger bones, dangling on long strips of hide, around their necks.

People sing as they eat. When their mouths are full they hum softly. Sometimes they get up and walk around the room.

There are people squatting around the edge of the firepit. Over the pit there's a hole bashed in the ceiling. There's another hole in the roof. Even though most of the smoke is escaping through the holes in the roof and the ceiling, the odors in the room are overpowering. The songs of the cannibals mingle and sound like a single, ornate musical line.

I am afraid they are looking me over, sizing me up as a future sacrifice. Four people across the room are sitting, staring at me, gripping their ears. I'm not sure what the significance of that is, but it scares me. Also, a man stands on the other side of the fire from where I sat with the triplicates. His face is obscured by the rising smoke and the heatwaves coming from the pit. They are most certainly considering eating me. They are trying to assess my power. Too many people are paying attention to me. I want to interview the druggist before I leave, but I feel that I ought to get out of this house as fast as I can, without arousing the antipathy of my hosts. I tell the three young men that the interview is over, "Thank you, thank you," and put my tape machine and camera back in the bag. I'm sweating like a pig. It's a touchy situation. I've got to be careful not to move too quickly or say the wrong thing. Everybody's looking at me. They're being subtle, coy about it.

Wrong door. It's a bathroom...no, it's just a tiled room with a drain in the middle of the floor. There's blood and hair splattered all over the place. The slaughtering table. Close the door. There's the front door. Nobody's following me. But they're all looking, peering around corners.

I manage to slip out—I'm back in the night. I got a little tape and several photographs, and I'm getting away without injury. Back up the hill, through the brambles and mud, up underneath the silent freeway. I am being tailed. Two men are following at a distance. Both of them are bare chested, in spite of the weather. I don't know whether these guys are planning to capture me, or what. So, I just keep plodding along, trying to keep my fears under control.

When I come back out on the other side of the freeway the men are gone. Standing under an arc-light, I check the bag to make sure my tools are intact. Everything's fine. I have to keep my eyes open—anything can happen out here. There're all kinds of hazards besides the cannibals. People become insane with hunger...just mindless. These are the ones to watch out for. They live in bushes, they stand waiting behind pillars. They'd rip a dog, for instance, to pieces. They'd eat the animal right there, under the lights, on the sidewalk. I've seen things like that happen. I keep walking. I'm coming out of a shallow valley. The sidewalk is broken in places. I remember when the streets were kept in perfect repair. I don't care anymore than anyone else; it's just typical of the era. I'm catching as many details as I can for the archives. Just the small amount of tape and the few pictures I got tonight were well worth the risk and the effort. I also managed to slip away with a few small bones and another skin armband.

Somewhere nearby, in one of the houses that line the thoroughfare, someone is using an electric food grinder.

1982

Our Moon of Moons

The gastric disturbances of the unnatural and bloated night bubble and smoke in our dreams. A severed limb here, a blood red crescent there.

The highways glower, evaporated. The traffic exhumed and shifted backwards in its tunnels. Clouds of abandoned putrescence hanging over the pavement.

The dome of air over the inhabited part of the land a sickly yellow and glowering stomach with the esophagus dimly lit, the gullet propped open with painful surgical stilts and aimed at a blank, artificial light.

The fluids of digestion work on our crushed and twisted features, causing our faces and hands to ooze into the bedding. Yet, we wake with a struggling sense of identity, run to the mirror, the blank wall, actually, and say, "Yes, yes, it's all there, still there."

But, it's not yet morning. It's never morning. The ceiling lights up, there are noises and we take that as a sign to begin—to digest and to be digested, horribly, breaking down and being broken down to a limpid sauce that swirls at the bottom of the dish and is sent back untasted.

We are engaged in the work of joyless eating and are, ourselves, gulped down thoughtlessly, regurgitated as puffed up and misshapen images of ourselves, as we too spit the knives and tasteless shards of our realities as a rosy and more palatable food for our senses, an ever more bland and mucousal soup. In the blackness beyond the moon the weary clink of surgical instruments working the lacerated and festering mouth of our really all too small universe. In the end the surgeons behind their steamy masks and caked in blood and dripping with vile green excretions will sew the thin discolored lips together to prevent the further poison of speech and gobbling of monumental excrement.

The light of sun and moon blink out and there is an absolute frigidity, a silence from which all meaning has been sucked, baking horribly in our darkling sky.

The signs go blank and wiggling as under tons of black rancid earth we open our dripping maws and suck at fat dollops of manure and decaying meat. Our kitchens are blind places of linoleum and faceless playing cards. Whimpering from children's bedrooms, we know not where, down which hall. Anyway, there is no longer the instinct to comfort, only to swallow in hunks the very substantial dark and silence of the sutured-shut body of the universe. Our little cities lost, cringing, separated, in the rubbery folds of the stomach—the thing now feeding on itself.

A terrible doctor holds up the remains by one leg howling: "This is the efficient means of extinguishing these things—sew up their orifices, their mouths and rectums, they will quickly exhaust the nutrients of their own flesh. The lifeless and skeletal remains of their celestial and spacial bodies may be of some interest, who knows?" We have made our way to the black and still pulsing diaphragm of the thing, our lips working as desperately hungry termites on the massive but helpless egg layer.

Our bedrooms are full of dust. A memory of sunlight pierces the blinds, casting harsh, dizzying stripes of long ago extinguished light on unused and disheveled furniture. An open wallet. Milk carton of piss next to the bed. Phone ringing and ringing. Hollow spider's shell still gripping the ceiling. All abandoned by the eater and the eaten, alike.

You will see your future, a black jam, slopped into its mold and watch, with a little hope, as it congeals. Then the job of gnawing through the chalky black trying to get at the tangled contours of your few precious tomorrows. Soaked in the bilious juices of your host and maker's gut, your skin slides from your body, your teeth narrow. Time deserts you and your remaining days harden and crack with the dry bones of your fingers scratching into their white prison. I can't continue. There is a rigid frost over everything. A plethora of grey weeds. Pink tongues tangled into a frightening but decorative knot on the wall in front of me, glistening with ice, my own breath clattering down on the table. And I exist at the place of maximum protection. Room 43, surrounded by warehouses. A forklift sits groaning on a loading dock. The moon is purplish black, a swollen epiglottis, wobbling unconsciously on the edge of suffocation. The rasping mumble of the refrigerator; a bag of grapes, cigarettes, pills. A door closes, a toilet flushes.

We are all going to fall dead any minute.

MAIN STREET USA

We are in America. The pain is bad. We use anesthetics.

In Disneyland there is a place called "Main Street U.S.A." Old time pinball machines that cost one cent, player pianos, singing shoeshine boys, friendly cops—a turn-of-the-century America that never was. I visited this place and was overcome by nausea. The unreality is dizzying. I sat on a bench in front of the barber shop. A marching band played in the distance.

This is the stuff they pound into you when you're little: "No matter what you think you see this is America. TV, hand-over-your-heart, Wednesdays crawling under the desks when the air raid sirens wail—driven by duty more than fear—teacher makes sure we all have our little fingers locked together right behind our heads, knees tucked up to our chins, then she crawls under her own desk. **Hand over your heart or I'll blow up the world.** All clear and it's back to work, cafeteria smells coming from the vents like nerve gas. Ours is the best country: There's no barbed wire except around the cattle and the criminals and the army and the towing lot and the airplane factory and the movie star's houses ...there's no barbed wire in America. There's a lot of concrete. America is encased in concrete molded in the shape of an enormous false history. This history has a face—Americans see this face when they close their eyes in prayer or death. **In God We Trust.** That god is the false face of America: a gory history wearing a noble expression. Look at the Christians: cheap suits, late model family cars, neutral haircuts, completely deodorized. They are made in the image of their god. The churches are suburban wet dream and stink of air freshener. The sort of temple in which the American god would feel at home. Twenty-two million people sunk in its body suffocating, inert, the flesh hardening quick. **Think America! Buy America! Dream America!**

The parade came into view, the band marching out in front, filling the heart of Main Street U.S.A. with the bright music of an imagined America. Brass instruments twinkled in the daylight...purple uniforms, flushed pink faces, white gloves. I watched them pass. After the band there was a long line of giant appliances—telephones, steam irons, radios—tooting, hissing, ringing as they marched. A parade of American inventions. Bringing up the rear were all the Disney characters—Donald Duck, Mickey Mouse, all of them. Watching all that big, noisy junk go by: Where was the giant sub-machinegun spitting spent cartridges, napalm with charred screaming victims, the atom bomb....This was the America rammed down my throat, shoved up my ass, stuffed in my ears, held glaring against my raw eyeballs in my childhood. The America I was raised to believe in. Daffy Duck and power mowers. Yahaaazuuuh! Yowwwwzzuhhh! Pop-pop-pop goes the shine rag. A banjo played somewhere down the street. I went into a store and bought a derby. Then I went to a bar and had a cream soda. A nuclear war could not touch this place. Main Street U.S.A.: the Safe Zone. Great palace of Fantasy Land glowing pink and blue in the distance. At night there would be fireworks. Davy Crockett would stroll in from Frontier Land and give a talk on fire safety. I went back to the bench with my cream soda and my derby and smoked a cigar. I was getting into the spirit of the thing, now. It was coming back to me. The flag, the virgin princess, Thomas Jefferson, all the glorious wars. I'm an American: everyone in the whole world loves me. Anyone who doesn't love me deserves to be killed. There is barbed wire around Main Street...to keep the cattle from wandering. The air is solid yellow-grey concrete.

In this setting it is easy to see what Jerry Falwell, Phyllis Schlafly, Nancy and Ron, et al, are thinking. These people never shed the crushing weight of early training. Cub Scout hat and fluffy party dress fused with the soft pink skin, can only be removed surgically. Very risky operation. Good luck. Through their eyes, here on Main Street, it makes good sense: disappear the poor, reduce all ideological discourse to one monotonous voice manipulated by soft invisible fingers, obedience enforced by blue steel tarantulas, styrofoam pioneer furniture, guns and plaster Jesus. Whisper from a drawer in the Doc's old roll-top: cops come and pull the thing out, smash it to pieces, burn everything. The owner is dragged outside, thrown into a deep hole and buried alive.

On other continents: Pueblo churchbells shot down by artillery; shaman's tongues sliced out by nine-year-olds in U.S. Army fatigues; Europe trampled again, turned to dark red mud covered with deep tread marks, boot marks, tire marks; all the hopeless ruins of the earth a dry dead pulp—vital juices have been drained into big tanks on the edge of Main Street U.S.A. Bones and wreckage make a 10,000 mile obstacle of death impassable by black rubber enemies. All ungodless dead.

Finally, only the twinkling of stars and the idle twirling of parasols. A young man runs out of the saloon and screams: "I want to be a girl!" He is shot down in the street by a pursed-lipped clergyman. Standing in the door of the soda shop, the mayor waves: "Good job, reverend. Got no use for those types on Main Street." Scream of the seltzer bottle.

It is all monotonous: the murder, the giant mice, the marching bands. It's a setup. Setup meaning everything is prearranged: the festive atmosphere, the killing, even the stars, everything that's said and felt here is rehearsed. Also, the clockwork life on Main Street is a setup for annihilation. Life on Main Street is the prototype for life all over America. Everything fits nice like a jigsaw puzzle—when the picture is done, it will be a picture of a sour empty planet. America has been a setup for suicide/global destruction from the start. Slaphappy clowns, lovable cops, politicians like take-charge dads from TV. We all fit into the picture puzzle somewhere. Guns to the temple, unbearable grinning—we'll get the signal.

I got up off the bench. The barbershop was closing. It was getting cold. I strolled off down Main Street U.S.A., following the inventions.

1986

Girl with Pizza

Our legs are touching. We're together. We're in love. Isn't he beautiful? He says I'm hot. Hot and heavy. I'm glad he likes me. I want to marry him. He says we're too young to talk about marriage. No-one's ever too young to talk about anything. At least he touches me.

My parents—especially my Dad—are over-protective. They underestimate my intelligence and they think I am a fragile little flower. Maybe it is because I am fat, maybe it is because I am quiet. But I know they are on my side. They just don't want me to get hurt, and they don't think I can look out for myself. I love my parents, even if they try and run my life.

As for what I think: It is too warm. I don't know why I'm eating pizza. I ought to be eating ice cream. I think I'll eat some ice cream next. I think I am a genius. I think I am a sex fiend.

That's what I think.

PIRATE

On this page of life there is a loaded gun. We are without blood, however. Our eyes are already dried up wounds. We have no sex. The gun will not shoot us. I wait to go to a movie.

Try and avoid memory. When love scenes surface they are like sea monsters ramming the boat and churning up the water. The foamy sea is chattering with broken ribs.

The movie is about pirates who believe there is something more valuable than gold. They board a ship, round up passengers, captain and crew, then they question everybody for hours. Meanwhile, the ship has gone off course, and no-one knows where they are, anymore. Whatever the pirates were after is now meaningless. They drift passionlessly to their deaths.

In my own life this takes the shape of a sordid country and western song. I write these when I can't stop grasping at the air. I grip a powerful weapon, hold it high and fire at the moon. Disembodied sobs ring out. It rains antlers representing freshly slain beauty and life. Then, I condemn love, uselessly, in a hollow voice.

Blood runs out my pants legs. At first I think it is only piss, but then I collapse on the carpet, my vision growing dim. Dream hands scour my eyesockets, replacing the eyeballs with glass marbles. Then, I know I am beyond death and love. If the woman comes back, I won't know her. If she says she loves me, I won't understand.

My heart carved in rubber will wind up in a museum, a curiosity. It was not worth getting lost at sea over. Hundreds perished. Miles of icy green water. Shattered ribs bobbing on the dancing peaks of the sea. An unrecognized, uncared for purgatory. My idea of a personal retreat.

1988

Window

Once when the wind did not blow I was filled with still panic. I opened the window wide, stuck my head out there and sucked at the air fiercely. It was as though my head were locked in a small, hot metal box, all the seams chalked with black rubber. The stiff, white sky turned darker and darker, the light sagging in the motionless air, coughing itself away into a dreary blackness. Runic characters, elaborate geometric patterns, images of mundane everyday objects appeared as lightning bolts against the hot pitch of suffocation. All the electric switches clicking on and off in a chattering riddle, the bright, soul-less chirping of insects; the harsh fur of the water left on. Crying in the squashy, bruised atmosphere. The wind had been dead nine minutes. My head hung out a ninth floor window, senseless. There was no traffic, no ship horns on the water.

"Your wife is downstairs, Clifford," said a man's voice rotten. "I guess she found you." My flimsiest parts began breaking. "Your wife is downstairs, Clifford. I guess she found you." Over and over like repeated announcements of an arrival at an airport.

The girl next door played scales on her trumpet. The Frye Hotel was full of musicians. This girl practiced four or five hours a day. I threw up into the airless void, and heard it, seconds later, splashing on the sidewalk. Do-re-mi-fa-so-la-ti-do. "Hey you, you're going to fall! Hey!" Do-re-mi-fa-so-la-ti-do. "Hey you, you're going to fall!" Do-re-mi-fa-so-la-ti-do.

Vision of a platinum wig. Screaming cannibals of the benevolent oligarchy. Everything I'd been trying to get away from. Inescapable. I fell forward heaving. The walls tightened, brutally inflexible. Shattered plaster. Bending bones and penetralia. Air thick as grey putty. Panic gripped at my ribcage and worked it like a frenzied squeeze-box. My legs shot out straight and I fell back jittering into the room. The sill tasted liked a banana. I bit down hard. Leaning back out the window I spit splinters of wood and paint chips. A cry filled my chest but stopped at my throat. My mouth worked silently. I felt tears streaming down my face, but when I touched my cheeks with my hands they were dry. The girl played "I Got Rhythm." The sink ran. A big wheel went round and round like a ferris wheel; I got sick, again. The puke hit the cement. To me: "Get your head back in there." To someone else: "That place is full of dope addicts." I leaned forward. If there had been a wind it would've held me up; it would've sung to me; it would've carried me away. But the sky was dead still. Dead.

"Clifford." She knocked. "Clifford." She knocked, again. "Clifford, it doesn't matter." She rang the buzzer.

It doesn't matter. The trumpet next door stopped. My head filled with bloody, steam smeared light. My body sagged over the window frame, creased painfully at the belly. Moving my lips, but without making a sound, I said: "My only friend is gone. Died. A few minutes ago my friend died." And a still but violent pressure built around me; a thing that was the opposite of a wind—the dense and unimaginably huge corpse of a wind. The whole firmament, bruised and squishy, had collapsed over the planet like a blue-black pudding. Still, the sink. And, Pajamas knocking.

"I don't want anything. I just want you to open the door and talk to me." Yes, that was the old voice that had always opened my doors.

"Talking. Opening the door. That's not nothing—that's something very big," I thought, pulling down the drapes with my red fists.

I thought of Phillip, too, suddenly for the first time in minutes, since the wind had died and the monotony of death clamped over my face like a door and sealed shut. Phillip and Pajamas. They belonged together, I guess. But, you can pick any two people at random and say that about them and be right. Phillip was a friend of mine—a close friend, in fact. He had stood at the door, too, knocking and knocking, and saying friendly and comforting things. I finally let him in. That was an hour ago ... maybe half an hour, I don't know. We sat in two chairs by the sink, by the little table with the hot plate and the dishes and the utensils, and talked quietly around what it was that really needed to be talked about. And, in the end, feeling that I had to say something very clear about his affair with Pajamas, I picked up a long, heavy kitchen knife off the table, jammed it in between Phillip's ribs and twisted it. I killed him in such a spontaneous, ordinary and half-minded way that he didn't even notice what I was doing. He lapsed into a little seizure like thing, twitching and spitting blood, then he fell forward into my lap. I stood, leaving the front half of his body resting face down on my chair, blood squirting from the wound in his chest, and from his mouth, onto the bare carpet. Then, I walked, in the dying graying atmosphere to the window, and opened it wide.

"I know you're in there. I asked at the desk. I want to talk to you, Clifford. There's a light under the door. Stop playing." Her knock was hard and quick and exasperated. "Goddamnit. Jesus, open your door and talk to me."

"I used to say those same words, myself, in just that tone of voice—it didn't work for me, either," I thought. "And gentle pleading won't work, and threats won't work, and rational wheeler-dealering won't work, and 'let's be adults' about this won't work...."

The girl played "My Funny Valentine." This must have been her favorite song—she played it beautifully, especially well, better than she could play, in fact. It had been one of my favorites, too, when I still enjoyed music. Even now, I seemed to like her playing; but my pleasure was a wisp that I could not quite grasp. I listened, anyway, imagining myself moved in the old way. I squeezed my eyes closed tight and felt the little tears.

"Have you talked to Phillip? He said he was coming over here to see you. It wasn't easy tracking you down. We called every hotel in five cities. This isn't the worst thing that's ever happened, Clifford. We can make it right, somehow. You know that. But, we have to talk. Are you listening? Just tell me that you're listening." Pajamas stood silently outside the door waiting for me to answer.

"Make it right, somehow." In my mind the words were a harsh command. The girl had stopped playing. The sink was a nagging, grating, constant sound that for some reason I could not think of a way to silence. The insect sound hummed and sang and twinkled in my ears. I realized that the heavy, close box around my head was the room; that Phillip's freshly murdered corpse was pressed tightly against my face. There was no-where to go. The room was encased in the density of the world around it, as though in tons of solid concrete; my head was smothered between the walls of the room; and my body was lost. My torso hung unfeeling out the window. My eyes blinked. I saw only a shadowy blur. There was a cruel swaying of justice. The entire mass of all that I knew of the world—indeed, of all worlds—began to list dizzily.

"Clifford, I can't just stand here. If there's something wrong...." Her voice died.

"No, there's nothing wrong, Pajamas," I said out loud, and fell forward out the ninth floor window of the hotel. The dead grey air suddenly lit up and stirred into a bright wind. And, as I had known it would, the wind held me up and sang to me, and carried me away to this sinner's heaven.

Pajamas stood knocking on the wrong side of the door.

1986

SLIDES FROM WINTER VACATION

The eye with its painful rose shudders in a rush of sweating panic riddles as the winter war sweeps by.

I always see the war as vacation slides. We sit together, you and me, in the dark, a dagger on the wall, gun stashed under the cushion, big white bowl of popcorn, bottles of 7-Up. "There's an old one of Pol Pot doing his cigarette trick." And we double over in a fake machinegun attack. Mick Jagger singing *"Ti-i-i-ime is on my side, yes it is."* US green berets giving torture lessons to government troops in El Salvador, hamming it up with severed body parts, mimicking the contortions of half dead prisoners. *"You'll come runnin' back, you'll come runnin' back to meeeee."* Soldiers desert to Mexico holding their stomachs still choking on the smell of burnt flesh. Next is just a bullet hole in a foreign billboard. A stray. Bullet whizzing around the world nicking every human and every image of humanity. Finally, we'll all be slightly wounded and everything that is ours will be a little broken. Buzz gun encased in future ice will reveal to scientists the source motivation of modern war dropped from brittle fingers into waxy toilet mud. "Angel, hand me the bottle." Glistening helicopters cutting through the mist strafing a beach of shouting Libyans. Dripping fangs painted on one. Treetops zipped off like hot whiskers. Flashing to the interior with its stone temples and houses made of weeds. A heap of beat tires with squirming girl. Everything seen from the air. China, South America, Southeast Asia. Winter has hit and the shadows of bones hide every continent. Wiggling in a cage of woven intestinal meat. Ice twinkling on shoulders. Breathtaking. Pair of pajamas frozen in a barren field; sleeping man fled to Mexico with memories of tortured grandmother, lurid

Americans eating canned food over her broken corpse. His dream needs a bandage. Hardened medical team at work. Unopened cigarettes on the coffee table. "Light me a smoke hon." City on fire. Running secretaries and exterminators and private detectives swept away and delivered to the ash wall nailed to the undersides of the clouds. *"Try to set the night on fiiiiire."* "Wait, it's lit crooked....There." I'm handing you the cigarette. "We could've gotten a real marble tabletop for the same price." "There's Idi Amin's mansion in Saudi Arabia. Whole thing made of shinbones and hair." The big inky man smiles in the shade of a stone elephant. Desert crocodiles wrestle at his feet. A whole war lies mummified in subterranean chambers. The screen lights with these stark arc-lit scenes. Man with mining helmet hunkers over decayed weapons and small dusty hands. Faces have been deliberately rubbed off. He takes a small caliber automatic from inside his shirt and fires point-blank into a slim powdery torso. Orange gel oozes from the holes. Picture of the man grinning, his helmet cockeyed. "We are lucky to have this machine." "And it wasn't expensive." I stick my hand into the couch and touch the big .45. Tactical nukes erase corners of war with spot-welding precision. The icy craft of computer warfare, a dazzling intricate pattern of purplish light seen from space and recorded a hundred thousand exposures per minute. "Wonderful, spectacular." The ground is left pitted and buzzing. No sign of anything having ever happened there. This appears on the screen first as an exotic glowing mollusk, then a whispering field of fine dirty white powder. Actual fighting is shouted down by imposing the sudden nonexistence of combatants, territory, cowering infants and all confused humanity. I am especially fond of this picture since it transcends conflict and shows the ultimate clean and mechanical dot-to-dot warfare. Explained by the wandering stray—the bullet has touched everything at this point and expanded its attack on humankind to include all life, and indeed much of the non-living planet, as well. "It's so flat." "It's exciting." "Painted, painted, painted, painted black." The screen goes dark and fingers of ice dangle at the edges. "Let's go back to the beginning." Here the sun shines and groups of men approach one another screaming with long wooden forks and bludgeons. Children are hidden under piles of leaves, the old look on weary, women of all ages stand brave and motionless in low narrow doorways. Obsidian dagger jammed up under the ribs. The first to die. Clattering of wood and stone. Death howls. Slashed arteries spraying blood at the sun. The trampled grass is hidden from the sky by pierced and broken bones and fat and muscles. Now a slide of a sad village overrun by the thirsty victors. The old executed on the bare yellow earth. Girls raped and kicked under a thin passing cloud, dragged off by the throat. Not a man alive. These are thrilling and colorful photos with wild jazz of the early-70s. Unexpected slide: me in mudsoaked pants shirtless with fast smoking gun and dead naked coolies sinking into the ferns. Proud of this one. "There's me, babe." It was a quick kill. "You look really mean." I grab at the gun in the couch, but she gets there first, puts her hand around mine. "Not that mean." We drink 7-Up, burp, watch the screen through the glass bottles. "Yell like you yelled when you killed those guys." "I killed them with my mouth closed." "Close your mouth like that." Lips like a slice in dry white fruit. "Oh, that looks very hard." Thinking of the computer at war my whole brain hard and tightened around annihilation, searching on the keyboard monitor for something moving, looking for me. Painting out section after section of the planet's colorfully splotched and lined skin. Mouth sealed, smooth forehead, eyes dry and dull. Poking at the keys with a pointed stick. This picture. I am not mean. This is my game. Going to war is a vacation. Take the camera. Bring it home. I have a big collection. You come over to see my collection. "Stop the show I have to go to the toilet." Turn on the lamp. The screen goes grey. Chew a handful of popcorn. Take out the gun. Fat heavy blueblack weapon. Very clean with perfect little parts. Clip loaded with stubby penis-like cartridges, nickel jackets, big lead slugs. One in the chamber. Click off the safety. There is also the war between you and me. I'm going to win this war, a war you are not conscious of, but that exists all the same between me and you and me and everyone else. The bathroom door opens and closes. Running water. Turn off the lamp and switch on the projector. *"You-ooo-ooo-ooo send me, darling you-ooo-ooo-ooo send me."* Picture of a dimly lit tunnel under Cu Chi, Viet Nam. Very tiny. Mexican with a .45 and a flashlight sweating, poking the walls and ceiling for booby traps, edging along in sneakers, squeezing through the slender hole in the steamy darkness looking for a small enemy. "I thought you were going to wait." "I'm waiting. This is it." "This is what?" "That's my gun." "The one in the picture?" "This is the same gun." Take the gun out from under my leg. "Can I see it?" Turn on the lamp. Point the gun at your face. "Look at it this way. Look into the hole." Fascinated like a snake, head bobbing, eyes crossed. "It's hypnotic." "The war's over for you." I hold my arm rigid and ball up my hand, finger slowly closing around the trigger. "Are you killing me?" "Yes, yes." A whisper. Flash and deafening report. Your face is smashed open, blacked and bleeding, you lurch back hard and quick and collapse frothing on the couch. This is how to fight a war: by guile and hypnosis with a single bullet in the livingroom. Go for the camera. Gun next to my empty 7-Up bottle. I take a drink of yours. Shots from every angle. Drive you to a deep tangled canyon. Wars never stop. The soldiers bring them home and continue to fight them hardly noticed. Turn off the music and the projector. Wait for the enemy. Make an enemy out of you. I have a photograph of you.

Car Accident

TORE UP CAR WITH SHELF PAPER AND BLOOD AS THOUGH AN ANIMAL HAD BEEN BUTCHERED INSIDE. MAN IN OILY COVERALLS, MUSTACHE AND THIN HAIR RAISING THE BELT AND BRINGING IT DOWN: "YOU BAD SONOFABITCH. YOU BAD BAD SONOFABITCH." BANGING ON THE GRIMY HOOD. YELLOW FIELD WITH OILSTAINS, PIECES OF BLACK MACHINERY. THE MAN STOPS, BOTH ARMS SORE, TURNS TO THE ROAD. ACROSS THE ROAD A SMALL GREEN HOUSE. THE SKY SULPHUROUS GREY, SMOKEY. INSIDE THE HOUSE, NEAR THE FRONT WINDOW, A WOMAN'S BODY ON A SMALL BLACK COUCH, HER HEAD AND ARM IN THEIR RIGHT PLACES, BUT SEPARATED FROM THE BODY BY GOOEY PURPLE-BLACK LINES. THE MAN POUNDS THE HIGHWAY WITH THE BELT AS HE WALKS TOWARD THE OPEN DOOR OF THE HOUSE. THE AIR STINKS OF GASOLINE. THE TANK HAD BEEN SHEARED OPEN AS THE CAR JUMPED THE GUARDRAIL, SPLASHING GAS ALL OVER THE HIGHWAY, SOAKING THE WHITE WEEDS.

HE SITS ON A BIG BROWN CHAIR ACROSS FROM HER AND SWITCHES ON THE RADIO. A LURID SONG ABOUT A BAR IN COLORADO, A LADY AND A MURDERER. HEAVY GAS FUMES DRIFT IN THROUGH THE OPEN DOOR. THE RADIO MAKES A SOUND LIKE DARK URINE. THE LADY IS WITH A MAN; THE MURDERER KILLS THE MAN; THE LADY LEAVES THE BAR WITH THE MURDERER; IT'S RAINING; THE DOOR SLAMS. THE ARM ROLLS OFF THE COUCH ONTO THE CARPET. THE BLOOD IS DARK AND RUBBERY AND MAKES A MARK LIKE A CRAYON. THE MAN GETS UP FROM THE CHAIR, GOES OVER TO THE

COUCH, PICKS UP THE ARM AND PUTS IT BACK ONTO THE BODY. HE TURNS THE HEAD SO IT IS FACING HIM, GOES BACK AND SITS ON THE CHAIR. SOUND OF A MAN HOLLERING AND BEATING THE CRAP OUT OF HIS FAMILY; A DULL VOICE SAYS, "DRUNKS AREN'T FUNNY." THEN: "IF YOU HAVE BEEN TURNED DOWN BY OTHER INSURANCE COMPANIES, IF...." THE MAN TURNS THE RADIO DOWN AND LOOKS INTO HIS WIFE'S FACE. HE IS ALONE IN THE GREEN HOUSE; THE HIGHWAY IS SILENT; HE HAS AN ORANGE HEADACHE FROM BREATHING GASOLINE.

"SO, WHAT DID YOU GET IN TOWN, SHIRLEY? I SAW YOU GOT SOME SHELF PAPER. IT LOOKS JUST LIKE MAPLE WOOD. IT'S ALL OVER THE BACK SEAT. WHY IS IT ALL OVER THE BACK SEAT? YOU MUST BE TIRED. YOU JUST LAY THERE. I'LL MAKE DINNER TONIGHT." THE MAN GETS UP AND GOES THROUGH A DOOR. HE STANDS IN THE MIDDLE OF THE KITCHEN LOOKING AT THE STOVE, THE REFRIGERATOR, THE CUPBOARDS, THE SINK. THE THROWUP LINOLEUM IS THIRTY FEET DOWN. THE MAN IS DIZZY FROM LOOKING AROUND THE KITCHEN. "WHAT'S FOR DINNER, SHIRLEY?" HE GOES BACK IN THE FRONT ROOM AND SITS ON THE BROWN CHAIR.

THEY HAVE THEIR OWN GASOLINE PUMP. YOU HAVE TO REMEMBER TO TURN THE VALVE OFF UNDER THE HOUSE WHEN YOU'RE THROUGH USING THE PUMP. THE WHOLE HOUSE STINKS OF GASOLINE. "HOW'M I GOING TO IMPRESS ON YOU THE IMPORTANCE OF TURNING THE VALVE OFF, SHIRLEY?" THE MAN LOOKS AT HER WITH THIN, DARK LIPS. "UNDER THE HOUSE IS ALL FLOODED." HIS FINGERS TURN WHITE. "HOW'M I GOING TO TEACH YOU...SHIT." HIS EYES SPIT. "ANSWER ME YOU STUPID CUNT!" HE JUMPS UP, GOES OVER AND SLAPS HER IN THE FACE. THE HEAD ROLLS OFF THE COUCH AND FALLS ON THE CARPET, WITH A COLD BUMP. "YOU CAN'T USE THE GODDAMN CAR, ANYMORE," HE YELLS AT THE PURPLE JELLY STUMP OF HER NECK, ACCIDENTALLY STEPPING ON THE HEAD, AS HE MOVES CLOSER. THE MAN LOOKS DOWN AT HIS FOOT, LIFTS IT CAREFULLY OFF THE HAIR, EAR AND CHEEK OF THE HEAD, BENDS OVER, PICKS THE THING UP WITH HIS SCARRED AND DIRTY FINGERS, AND PUTS

IT BACK ON THE BODY SO IT IS LOOKING AT HIM. "I'M SORRY. I HAVEN'T HIT YOU ONCE, SINCE I QUIT DRINKING."

HE STANDS UP, TURNS, AND WALKS TO THE KITCHEN. HE GOES STRAIGHT TO THE REFRIGERATOR, OPENS IT, AND TAKES OUT A GREAT BIG STEAK. HE CLOSES THE REFRIGERATOR DOOR, WITHOUT BANGING IT. THE MAN PUTS THE RED STEAK ON THE MINT GREEN TILES. HE OPENS A CUPBOARD, TAKES OUT A FRYING PAN, PUTS THE HUGE STEAK IN THE FRYING PAN, AND PUTS THE PAN ON THE BURNER. HE OPENS THE CUPBOARD OVER THE STOVE AND TAKES OUT A BOX OF KITCHEN MATCHES. THE MAN TAKES A MATCH OUT OF THE BOX AND TURNS ON THE GAS. STRIKING THE MATCH, HE THINKS, "I FORGOT TO GREASE THE PAN."

THE SHELF PAPER FLAPS IN THE COLD WIND FROM THE OPEN CAR WINDOW. THE CAR, THE BLACK MACHINERY, THE WHITE GRASS ARE COVERED WITH TWINKLING FROST. THE ICY HIGHWAY GLOWS UNDER A WINTER MOON. ON THE OTHER SIDE OF THE HIGHWAY, FROZEN ASHES AND BENT PLUMBING WILL DISAPPEAR UNDER THE FIRST SNOW.

1987

PLEASURE ON PLATFORMS

(FOR THE COMING GENERATION)

yesterday, i found a real hot porn magazine in the waste basket in a filling station bathroom: "turned on teens. the coming generation." i was waiting for my ten year old son to finish with the toilet.

his mother (my ex) was out in the truck with barry and lea, joey's younger brother and sister (not mine). we'd been sitting there in the parkinglot drinking and talking while the kids fought it out in the back for a couple of hours.

joey had started to crap his pants so i took him over to the filling station to finish and get rid of his underwear. meanwhile, i pissed in the sink...no self control. after washing my hands, while throwing the paper towels in the wastebasket, i noticed the bag. sort of casually, without taking it out of the trash, i looked inside. i stood up quickly. hot stuff.

"hey, go back to the truck joey."

"i gotta wash my hands."

"never mind that. go back to the truck."

"you gonna shit?"

"yeah, now go on back to the truck." he just stood there. "look, i can't shit with you standing around in here." he threw his underpants in the toilet and flushed them down. then he walked out into the sunlight. i locked the door.

"jesus, this is some *good* looking snatch." i had taken the magazine out of the wastebasket and was sitting on the edge of the toilet rubbing my crotch through my pants. the cloth was already warm. i undid my belt, snap, zipper and pulled my pants down around my knees. i wasn't wearing any underwear.

on the first page was a picture of a woman about 25 doing a very convincing 16 or 17. i was satisfied. i'd been looking at the same tired magazines for several months. somehow, the pictures seemed to get worn just from being looked at.

the next five pages of "turned on teens" were covered with pictures of the 25-year old teeny-bopper. in every picture she was wearing platform shoes. the title of this series of photos was: "pleasure on platforms." in most of the pictures the shoes were all she was wearing.

she had one of those sassy little faces, still a trace of babyfat under the chin, pouting lips. you know the type. you see them on saturday afternoons crowding the buses bound in or out of the suburbs. you try not to look at them because you're afraid they're going to read the sad horniness in your face. not just the girl, but everyone on the bus *will* see.

she'll start screaming. they'll all gang up on you: old women with shopping bags pelting you with cabbages and cans of tomato sauce. the bus driver radioing for the cops. beefy characters with teenage daughters of their own—white t-shirts, bowling league jackets, smell of sweat, deodorant, brylcream—pounding away at your face snarling. little kids kicking you in the nuts. a woman's arm, that's all you see—loose white flesh, tiny wristwatch, one fine hair growing out of a mole halfway between wrist and elbow, but otherwise hairless. on the end of the arm is a red hand wrapped tight around the fronds of a potted-palm. she's bringing the goddamn pot down on your head. a piece of the shattered thing cuts deep into your forehead, just missing your eye. you're spitting out blood and specially treated dirt.

"DON'T LOOK AT HER! DON'T YOU EVER LOOK AT HER!!!"

it's an uproar. you're lying on the floor in the aisle battered half unconscious making a weak effort to block a few of the shoes. tennis shoes, wingtips, silver high heel sandals, grimy work shoes, new shoes, old shoes, earthshoes, spiked football shoes...you're being attacked by a wild shoe museum—and since it's spring: garden tools. why not? some guy's rushing down the aisle. people are jumping out of his way. he's coming at you with a lawnmower.

"FUCKING CHILD MOLESTER!"

you manage to roll under a seat and out of his way. someone else clips your ear with a rake.

pantlegs, smelly socks, shimmering nylons hugging white legs ribbed with varicose veins. red toenails, bedroom slippers, bowling shoes, golf shoes, walking shoes, lounging shoes. you look at your own feet. they're just inches away from your face. you're scrunched up in a ball. child molester shoes?

something heavy gets you in the small of the back. a boot, maybe.

"SLEAZY SON OF A BITCH CREEP!"

you can't move, panting and all sweaty. you piss your pants. the wet spot spreads out warm up your belly and down your thighs. because of the way you're balled-up, you've got your nose in it. it's like being a baby again: wet and scared. the familiar stink.

all the feet, the hollering, the pain; it's all receding, dying, growing dim. you stuff your thumb in your mouth and start sucking away at it. a little tinkling music box. mommy's winding it up now. tales of the vienna woods played by a small metal spool with fingers on a piano the size of a book of matches. all the shoes look like trinkets hung over your crib. one of them catches you under the chin. a man's teeth dig into your thumb: your teeth. you swallow the salt.

close your eyes,

baby, and dream....

jacking off in a gas-station bathroom looking at pictures of a 25-year old 16-year old wearing only a pair of platforms shoes. god she's hot. the kind you make a point of looking away from on the bus.

i tore a long strip of toilet paper off the roll and wadded it up. i was just about ready to cum.

"dad? hurry up. barry got out of the truck and we can't find him."

i disguised my voice, trying to sound like i was taking a nice calm shit—got all the sweat out of it. "just a second, joey, i'm almost done. you keep on looking. i'll be right there."

i wadded up the toilet paper in my right hand. i always jerk off with my left: a true southpaw. the interruption had nearly cost me my hardon, but i soon conjured it up again. now where was i? that's right: i'm licking one of those small, hot nipples. then: she's giving me a touchingly amateurish blowjob. she's trying to be careful with her teeth. her lips, wet and slightly cool, are sliding slowly up and down my cock. she's exploring it with her tongue. she has a slightly shocked, intense expression on her face. she can hardly believe what she's doing. she pulls back and kisses the rigid head of it, then puts her mouth over it and swallows as much of my prick as she can, goes down until she gags. her eyes are closed. suddenly her face relaxes. she opens her eyes and looks up at me as i cum. she makes a small choking noise, like someone coughing with a mouthful of food, and sucks hard, gobbles it up and swallows it.

i set the magazine on the edge of the sink just in time to catch the cum in the ball of toilet paper. the magazine slid down toward the drain as i finished myself off.

"dad! dad! barry's hiding in the dumpster. he won't come out."

"ok. ok. hold on. i'll be there in a minute. just relax."

i took the magazine out of the sink and slipped it back in the bag. threw the sticky ball of paper in the toilet. pulled up my pants. zipped, snapped and belted them shut. flushed the toilet. lit a cigarette while i waited for my hardon to fully dissappear. walked out with the bag tucked carefully under my arm. the dumpster was about ten feet from the bathroom door. joey was chinning himself on the edge, peering in at his little brother.

"he's in there."

"all right barry, get your ass out of there immediately."

"fuck you, you smelly fart."

"here, hold this." and handed the bag to joey.

"what is it?"

"never mind. don't open it." and dove into the dumpster. i pulled barry out of the trash by the ankles. a blue paper towel was stuck to his t-shirt.

joey hadn't looked in the bag. it wasn't obedience, you understand. he was just more interested in watching barry and me fighting it out in that trash bin. it was a good fight.

"here, give me that." with my right i took the bag from joey, while i hung on to barry's arm with my left. (southpaw, remember?) the three of us walked around the fence and back to the truck in the parkinglot behind the elite.

in the front seat, on the passenger side, anna fed the baby some yogurt.

"what'd you buy?" she asked, looking at the bag.

"some porn. i found it in the wastebasket in the mens room." she knows me well so there was no reason to be embarrassed. i wasn't.

"oh. we're out of beer." i put the porn under the driver's seat and got back out of the truck.

i opened the backdoor of the tavern and went inside. at the bar i noticed several women, all around 25 and wearing platform shoes. it was heart-rending, i thought. this whole row of women, all friends, working so goddamn hard at sixteen and coming out around fifty. they were all worn out. i looked at one of them and smiled. it's safe now. nobody cares who smiles at these women.

i bought my beer and went back to the truck.

1979

Sunday Execution

I'm not afraid anymore. Only a few years ago, in this same situation, I would've been a wreck. I'll tell you what makes all the difference: experience, preparation. You see what I look like...it used to be very hard for me to face certain situations. I was in this very spot in 1982, right here, and I froze up, I was really terrified. We had to call it off. It took three years of intensive training, going through all the motions over and over, before I had the nerve to try it again. Now, here I am, entirely confident. I feel great. They have coaches who specialize in training people for this kind of event. They teach you to turn your fear and anxiety into excitement. You learn to handle increasingly stressful situations gracefully, even eagerly. In most cases it takes a few months, maybe a year, but I'm such a nervous person, so timid, it took me awhile to get ready for this. Standing here, today, I feel only the thrill of anticipation. I realize it's five o'clock in the morning; you'd like to get this over with, wouldn't you? Okay, I just wanted you to know that I'm really ready this time. We don't even need to use the blindfold. I'll just stand over here against the wall, and...this is so exciting! Alright, go ahead.

After TV

The airwaves are dead. Turning the channel selector, nothing but hissing and whistling and crackling silver.

The movies peter out one after the other.

On one channel it's a grand colonial mansion surrounded by weeping willows and birch trees. A fat black woman with a rag tied around her head stands on the porch waving sadly with one hand, while dabbing her eyes with a handkerchief held in the other. Moving towards us and away from the house and the crying woman, down a narrow lane under the willows: a carriage driven by a young white gentleman. By his side is a young white lady, dangerously frail, in a swoon of potent but courteous ecstasy. Piled in the back of the carriage are several suitcases and a lamp. The carriage, its two passengers and their luggage are rolling slowly, bobbing romantically into the foreground: filling the screen, filling our eyes, rolling into the future, rolling into our smoky insomniac bedrooms. The old woman—we see her now through a small, dusty oval window over the tops of the suitcases—is pulling away, is being sucked backwards into the thin scummy funnel at the back of the picture tube. Down the drain. Tinier and tinier. A speck of black fuzz on the camera lens. She is no longer a woman. She is no longer crying. All that's left are the inflated faces of the two young travelers, rosy and sparkling. Perfect fresh pastries; tender and sweet and gooey. Shit. The end.

On another channel it's 1951. That gray year. A group of witnesses are filing out of the death chamber of a penitentiary. So dour and pale! They seem to be suffocating in the solemn atmosphere of justice. Or is it the stink of burnt hair and flesh and steaming urine that's got them gagging? And, no doubt, the charred corpse in the other room was once a lovable character. They spent the whole movie telling us how, even though he was a brutal murderer, the man who'd just been executed wasn't really such a bad guy. As a matter of fact he was a regular hero. Yes it's plain that someone whom everyone loved, but wished dead all the same, has just been fried. Well, that's the rules, bub. We got to play by the rules. Some love. Some rules. Cut to a shot of the chair—empty with its dangling leather straps, its steel buckles and sooty skullcap. The end.

And now it's time for the news wrap-up. This is the last and final word, folks. Here's where we get the lowdown, here's where they tally up the scores: the wars, the accidents, the muddles, why life is going to be intolerable in about three years and what a bunch of fat, drunk worried looking assholes are going to do about it. Of course it's a fixed match. And by this time, I'm too numb to be impressed even by the suffering, the deaths of millions of people. What the fuck do I care? Don't they know it's dark out there? I can't even see the trashcans overflowing out in the driveway; how can they expect me to see a bunch of dead bodies floating in a river 10,000 miles away? Jesus. Look. I've got $3 and a can of kippers. So, fuck all you spectral children with your shivering bellies and your eyeballs blistered by napalm. And fuck your gook nigger mothers, too. Let them suck clappy cock until they choke to death, spitting pus from their nostrils. Let your sobbing fathers shrivel up into bamboo birdcages, crawling with maggots. It's not my goddamn problem.

God, I don't mean that! None of it! But I don't know what to do.

Well. Then we get the sports and the weather. I'm sweating in my blankets, believe me, I want to know what's going on here. Baseball scores and hockey scores and golf—God, I hate golf—and a picture of the world taken by a robot, a machine run by batteries humming away in space. You look at that picture, that faraway ball of candy: how do I know that's my planet, huh? Show me my street, show me my house.

Yeah, the juice goes up and down in the thermometer. All those little numbers...the clouds swirling down over Alaska.

But we're still not through! There's more! Yes! The man with gray hair—a twirl, a smoky French doughnut coif hovering over his head—a pudgy, self-righteous pussy of a man sitting casually (as if to say: "I'm just one of the boys.") on the edge of a desk in a fake studio set office. He's going to give us the straight dope. He's going to tell us his opinion. He's going to explain why we shouldn't be mad at his roley-poley buddies who're sucking our guts out through our pockets. Shit. Is this the end? Not quite.

Now there're the jet fighters and gold meadows and seagulls and black smokestacks of America. "...and the land of the free...." Zzzzzz.

Then all the local stations are dead, the TV picks up a faint signal from a few hundred miles away: a religious broadcast. More slick talk. Sweet mouth gangster type—coming straight out of Fort Worth, Texas, huh?—and his faithful colored side-kick, their cuff-links flashing, their foreheads glistening under the hot studio lights.

Now, I really heard this....I saw those two hombres on my TV set and they were really saying this: that they would, absolutely free of charge, acting solely out of a sense of Christian duty, (now dig this...) help us to make out our wills. Yes, even in death we will be able to support God's work. "Our counselors are waiting to take your call." Those boys in Fort Worth....God's servants....

Then more news and another chummy wise-ass. "...and the home of the brave." Zzzzzzzzzzz. That's it. The old Indian-head target. Bingo! Zzzzzzz.

After television there are the birds, shouting and singing and laughing in the gray dawn. The birds and the police cars buzzing the streets looking for criminals, switching their blue lights and their sirens on and off. The police and the criminals...the birds yakking at each other.

Somewhere nearby, on top of a phone pole, there's a transformer that buzzes all night long. For whatever reason, you can't hear it until all the TV stations have gone off the air. The transformer's job is to push words through the wires. It doesn't care whether anyone's talking or not; it just keeps pushing. A whole river of alphabet soup. Old blabbermouth bitches...nervous junkies scratching their poor, sore arms...pimps, itching for death & money...poets dialing with shaky, calloused fingertips....Here I am saying all these words. All I'd have to do is say them into the phone and the transformer would push them all the way around the world, shove them into some chink's ear. Ha-ha.

Another 15 minutes and it'll be time for the morning report.

1979

Burnt Up Baseball Head

The frog healer helps herself to a death of tiny charcoal shames and penis rattles. We wait with evangelical poison in the whisper box of sullen swamp photographers and baby nail eaters. "Hey you burnt up old baseball head!" a boy yells from behind a greasy black thornbush. Old Frog Healer washes her face in a pool of brown muck. She turns her head. Her cheeks are soft and fresh. The boy runs like a confused and humiliated angel. "You lost your pants, sonny." She places a postcard from Wyoming face down on the surface of the pool and croons some old torch song as the picture gets soggy and heavy and starts to sink. The photo is an old woman standing on the endless plain with a giant baseball in front of her head. Frog Healer takes a small acetylene torch from her potato skin pouch, lights it, and holds the six thousand degree white flame to her face. Burnt up old baseball head ceremony. Ancient magic. The boy makes it back to America just in time to see his team lose. A black bush falls from the sky. There is an anal whispering in a hamper full of soiled underwear. The boy's mother is terrified. "He's no angel." "But, he's a virgin," wails the mother. "He's an evil cocksucker," cackle the drowned voices of the swamp photographers, in unison. "Johnny, get your poison little ass in here—the clothes hamper told me all about you." The sickening shit smell filled the air. "What's this smell, Mom?" "It's the truth. Now, tell me all about South America." "I lost my pants, okay? Now you know about South America." The boy glowed a brilliant acid green. "There's more, son, I can tell just by looking at you. Look at yourself!" She held up a serving platter. The boy saw a green snake with a greasy black thornbush. The sky was angry brown. "There was an old woman with filthy eyes and a purple mouth. When she spoke the snails stood up on their hind legs and whined. I was immediately attracted to her. What was I supposed to do? I chased her deeper and deeper into the swamp. Finally, we came to a place where many photographers had come to rest. "Anal pedagogue!" the old woman hollered, and all the photographers jumped out of the shit. The old woman looked all the more beautiful with those slimy cadavers dancing around her. Later, when we were alone...well, you know, Mom...you know what we did. When it was over my peepee thing was all grimy and shriveled up, I ran like hell. I forgot my pants. When I woke up I was holding a camera, wearing khakis and a bush hat. I was thirty-five years old. My muscles were starting to atrophy. I took a photograph of two platypuses going at it in the mud. But, when I developed the picture it was an old woman with a baseball in front of her head. I ran out of my tent screaming. I was really scared. I took an acetylene torch from maintenance and burned up the picture. Six thousand degrees is hot. There was nothing left but black dust. I was relieved. Next thing you know, though, there's the old hag in the bushes. I wake up again and I am eight years old without my pants and I am starting to piss all over myself. "Hey you little wise-ass, you better plug your ears." Suddenly, millions of snakes and leopards screamed. Above me vines and treelimbs shattered like crystal; birds fell upside down and stuck in the ground like metal pokers. The old woman's eyes looked like point blank range gunshot wounds—powder burns around the edges, purple jelly in the middle. She stared out of a black bush. I lost my sense of direction, my equilibrium. I fell to my knees and threw up. Her laughter was everywhere. "That's what you get when you fuck the Frog Healer, sonny." Everywhere frogs began to chirp, happily. I remembered the photo in my sleep. "Hey you old burnt up baseball head!" Old Frog Healer put her face in a mud puddle...washed her face in dirty water. But, when she turned around and looked at me she was fresh as a little girl...except there was this sarcastic leer. I ran, flapping my arms and crying. "I lost my pants, okay?" "Your father's going to tan your hide when he hears what you've been up to. Fucking old grandmothers, running around in the jungle without your pants on. You're in a lot of trouble, son." The boy went to his bedroom. He closed the door and sat on the bed. He took a book out from under the bed: *The Jungle Book.* There was a picture of a red frog. Under the picture it said, Venomous. There was also a picture of a green snake. The boy went to the mirror and held the book up next to his face. Looking at the book in the mirror he saw a picture of himself. Where he himself stood there was a green snake. He dropped the book. When his mother came into the room the snake bit her. She dropped dead on the beige carpet. The snake slid into her open pink mouth and down her throat. The poison doesn't actually take effect until after death. The mom drew up into the fetal position and turned crimson. Her eyeballs bugged out and turned black. Her pants suit caught fire and evaporated. Her body became limber and muscular and began twitching spasmodically. "Honey? Judy? Maybe she's out in the yard." Dad looked in the yard. "The TV in the kitchen's on." He looked in the den, the bathroom, and the bedroom. Then he looked in the boy's bedroom. "Nobody home. Funny...." A little red frog bit him on the ankle. "AHHHHH!! JESUS!!" Venemous. The book lay open, face down on the carpet.

1985

The Door

The door closed forever in the wind. That is, it closed over and over and over. The door, the doorframe and a small rotten floor stood alone by a long ago road. As the door hammered against the frame over and over, I saw, blinking in the sad, tin colored air a small, dreary room and a nude woman with sores on her legs drying herself in front of an iron stove. From an unseen chair in the orange darkness a man's voice said: "Aren't you going to close the door, Irene? Close the goddamn door!" Irene continued to dry herself. "If I have to get up off this chair...." She hung the towel on a nail and stood shivering in front of the black stove. A man appeared behind her so suddenly it looked like he was dropped into the picture from above. The man grabbed Irene by the hair and twisted her head around. "You mind me when I talk to you." Without letting go of her, he kicked the door shut. There was a still silence. The door creaked open a few inches, then blew open wide. The damp, rotten floor was bright and slick under the new winter sky.

I crossed the partly frozen ground to the warped grey-brown door and stopped with my arm raised, as though I was going to knock. I laughed a round puff of steam and let my arm fall back to my side. The door shook: I could hear the closed hollowness of a room on the other side. "You don't need to grab me like that. You keep treating me like an animal, I'm gonna turn on you like one, someday." "Well, you act like a goddamn animal. You got no *respect*, woman." The door opened suddenly; there was a gust of warm air as I peered into the lamp-lit gloom. "Goddamnit! " The door slammed shut in my face. "And, you don't have to swear all the time, Charles." I heard the hiss of faraway tires on the road and felt suddenly foolish and vulnerable. The wind made a pinging, knife-like sound as it blew around the edges of the doorframe and under the little floor. But, at that moment it was so large in my ears it seemed to be wearing away at the brittle corners of the earth. I stood shivering with my back to the road hoping the car would pass without its passengers noticing me, or that maybe it was on some other road. But the sounds of its engine and wheels grew closer. It must have been just around the bend, at the edge of the forest. The door opened with a tentative groan. On the other side were a light grey winter sky and frost green landscape. I stepped onto the spongy old floorboards and closed the door behind me. The thin scream of the wind was suddenly muffled and the sky was dimmed. The air around me was warm and smoky. "What do you think you're doing, just walking into my house? Get the hell out of here." Charles had jumped to his feet and grabbed a huge pistol off the end of the bed. "Oh, Charles, let the man warm himself by the fire. He isn't even armed, for God sakes. He's probably just lost, isn't that right, mister?" "Yes," I said. "Alright then, move over by the stove and get yourself warm." Charles sat back down on his grimy stuffed chair and put the gun back on the bed, taking care to place it within easy reach. I walked over to the stove and looked down at the shimmering air over the round iron plates. A big granite kettle sat off to one side. The heat penetrated the front of my pants and coat. I held my hands up over the stove.

"So which way are you coming from, Mr. what's-your-name?" Charles asked from his chair behind me.

"Bingham, and my name's Paul."

"There's no place by that name around here. Have you ever heard of a town called Bingham, Irene?" There was a suspicious hard squint in the pitch of Charles' voice.

"No, I don't believe I have," said Irene, in an odd tone.

"What year is it?" I asked, sounding distantly curious.

"Umm, are your hands warm yet, buddy...what-did-you-say-your-name was?" I could hear the springs in the chair as Charles leaned forward.

"Yeah, my hands are real toasty. My name's Paul." I could feel the gun looking at my back. Irene jumped up off the bed.

"Don't," she said.

"I'm not going to do anything. I just want to make sure he don't do anything." The man's voice was tense with fear.

"I'm not going to do anything," I said.

"You're a little touched in the mind, aren't you?"

"I'm alright, really. You want me to leave? I'll leave."

There was a long, dry silence.

"Where do you think you're going to go?" asked Charles.

"Right back up the road to Bingham."

"There's no such place, and there's no road, either."

"I don't think he's going to do anything, Charles. Why don't you put down that gun?" Irene knew her husband's quick, nervous violence; she felt a sad fear for the stranger.

"Alright, but you stay right there, where you are, by the stove, you hear me?"

"Yeah, I'll stay right here. I'll just warm myself up some more." I looked at the little things on the shelf over the stove. Greasy bottles, matches, a belt buckle, tin and granite pots.

"It's 1868," said Irene. Bingham was founded in the 1880s; the road was probably laid around the same time. Irene walked over to the big kettle, took a cup down from a nail on the wall, and poured out some coffee. "Want some coffee, Paul?" I looked at her without turning my head. She was studying my profile.

"Get the hell away from him."

"He's alright."

"I said get away from him."

I took the cup and stepped sideways, away from Irene. "Thank you." Irene backed away, out of my view.

"Never seen a coat like that," said Charles.

"No, probably not."

"Pretty fancy boots, too."

"Yup, they're good ones."

"Bingham, huh?"

"That's right, Bingham." I sipped at the sharp, brackish coffee.

"Take a look out that door," said Charles, suddenly loud and oily and righteous, like a preacher. "You take a look out there and tell me if you see a road."

"Alright." I walked to the door, opened it, and looked out. There was no road.

"You win, Charles, there's no road."

"Well then."

"Maybe he has a fever," Irene said, with some alarm.

"No, no, I'm fine, really," I said hurriedly, realizing what the word "fever" had meant in 1868.

"He's not sweating. His color's fine. He's just not right, that's what I think." For the first time Charles' voice betrayed something like genuine human worry for someone else.

"What do you think we ought to do, Charles?" Asked Irene.

"Well, I don't know. We can't just turn him out."

"Can't he sit down?"

"Sure, sure, give him a chair."

Irene dragged a wooden chair over to the stove and set it so it was facing the room.

"Go ahead, sit down," Charles said, with just an edge of harshness left in his voice. I turned around. Charles was a grizzled, worn out man, though he was, at the very most, forty years old. His hair was dirty and matted and looked as though he had been furiously tearing at it. He had short, bumpy limbs and what would've been a pot belly—but was a kind of deflated pocket of flesh that hung down over his belt line—were it not for the apparent scarcity of food and the overall hardship of his life. His face was mean and rumpled, cut and pounded by fear and struggle, the sleepless fight of frontier survival. Only a few snaggled yellow teeth showed behind his hard, brown lips. Charles' eyes were much bigger and rounder than I would've expected; they seemed to me to be the only thing he had been born with; they held themselves open with a brutal desperation and sucked greedily at the world. These were the eyes of a child who had been rarely fed, never loved, thrown early into the perilous arms of the elements with no warning or preparation. They were a child's eyes, even though they were veined and yellow and cruddy and pointedly threatening, and deeply threatened. A dark visor of animal shrewdness overshadowed his whole face. Beneath that was a great dense neck, like a weathered tree trunk, that held his head and his body together with a pure, unconscious determination. It seemed to be straining, trying to pull his head right down into the hollow between his shoulders. Charles' hands were small, hard, utilitarian things; pitted and twisted from years of resistance to, and constant contact with trees and stones and ice and animals and too much water and too much dust and withering heat and squinching cold—all the things that one survives both with and against; his hands were like iron keys which he fitted into the world—to unlock it for his petty plunder, to swing its big doors open—or to slam it shut and lock it tight when it, the world, screams too hard and cruelly against his life. His hands. Charles' feet were small, his cracked brown boots were small. The feet played with each other, bumping and bumping, working out Charles' thoughts there on the cold, splintery wooden floor.

"So, aren't you going to sit down?" He asked.

"Thanks." I sat down in the chair. Irene was sitting straight across from me, on the bed. She wore grey wool pants, a red twill shirt, beat up black half boots, no socks. Her hair was long and colorless and needed brushing, but it was clean and it seemed to crackle with inner electricity. She lifted a hand to draw the hair away from her face. Though the hand was battered, somewhat ruined by work and wear, and was almost gruesomely muscular, it belied an essential grace and gentleness and supple strength. I watched the hand rise, comb through the long strings of hair and settle, like a thing made of sand, on the bed.

Irene looked me over for a moment—her gaze was like a penetrating breath—then turned her eyes to the sweaty, grey window at the back of the cabin, next to the stove. Her ice-green eyes were slightly sour, not at all hard, not gullible, either, mystical as Druid charms, and though they showed the wounds of a life of abuse, Irene's were not bitter eyes, nor did they reveal a broken soul. I followed her eyes to the glass; long, gleaming eels of condensation cut their indecipherable symbols down the glazed and grey plane of beaded-up water. There was a slightly greenish cast to the light in the window, maybe because of the forest that began a few hundred yards from the cabin. Or maybe, I thought, Irene's gaze in some way affected the glass, tinting all the light in the sky. I turned my head so it appeared that I was looking at the dark, unpainted plank wall behind and between Charles and Irene. The boards were dry and splintery. There were no decorations on it, at all. I noticed this in an idle and unfocused way, since I was, in fact, still looking at Irene, at her legs and lower torso. She had the lithe build of a magical beast, like a doe in human form. But, she was certainly more hardened than her years would've normally suggested. This showed not in the lines of her body, or in the way that she moved, but in the hard burls of her knees, elbows and wrist-bones; her clothes hung on her body, as though on a carved statue. Still, there was a loose grace about even her smallest, unconscious movements, that came, it would seem, from living so much in her body. Her breasts were at the same time low and small. This struck me as being, somehow, truly exotic, incongruously bringing to mind women in filmy, lowcut gowns, holding martini glasses and long, silver cigarette holders. I imagined Irene for a moment in grainy black and white on the pages of a chic and expensive society magazine. The image grew cold and snapped out of focus. Irene put her hands between her knees and began cracking her knuckles as she continued to stare sidelong out the window, or—since there was nothing to see outside but the monotone snow and an indistinguishable wash of forest—at the window. The sound of her bones popping was like the sound of a clock made of worn out shoes and dead horses. Her journey ticking away behind a small, chilly window. She swallowed hard. Was it some regret, or was it hunger? A collection of thin, tasteless saliva swallowed as though it was what—wine? A piece of meat? A life of hardship that might've been something else? A forgotten man? She swallowed again. I could tell by the way her gullet moved—high and low, grasping at her pallet, throwing itself at her stomach—that there was nothing there, her mouth was dry and empty. I tried to discern what Irene was thinking and feeling by looking at her throat, for there was the softest, most revealing part of her. It was even another shade of skin; somehow unweathered, as though she had always kept it covered. Yes, there was a blind regret—blind, because she couldn't imagine what it was that she had missed. But, Irene knew that she had been born into the wrong life. Any hunger, any suffering at all, was dwarfed by this knowledge. Because she was preoccupied with another life—a life separated from her only by time—anything that might happen to her was like something that had happened yesterday or tomorrow, and to someone else. Irene turned suddenly and looked at me. Her eyes yawned wide. She moved back, pulled her legs up on the bed and leaned against the headboard.

"You oughtn't to put your shoes on the bed," said Charles, looking at her.

"Alright Charles." Irene turned so her feet hung off the edge of the bed. She looked at Charles with a vague and momentary sadness. Charles wasn't sure what he saw in her face. Mostly, he just saw 'plain Irene' when he looked at her, missing the emotive freight with which her expressions were so often laden. He only knew what she was thinking or what she felt when she told him—or when she cried or laughed or smacked him. He thought he saw some emotion expressed in the lines around her eyes, in the long drooping almond of her mouth when she said, "Alright Charles," but he wasn't sure, so he didn't say anything; he just coughed and turned his head. He looked at me and the stove. Irene went back to looking at the grey beads of moisture on the window. I looked at my knees. We sat in silence for a long while. There was only the muttering of the fire at the back of the stove, and the bright searing wind in the chimney—and these two almost universal voices said something different, I'm sure, to each of the three of us. For my part, I heard the boundaries of time teetering and heaving, tumbling into oblivion; ten thousand winters, both future and past, all in this very place, whistled and shivered and hissed and roared together, no longer held separate by the feeble and artificial fence-work of consciously divided time. What stood between one time and another? Events. And what stood between one event and another? Time. It was so easy, suddenly, to see it like that; to actually see all that has ever happened, and all that ever will happen as one and undivided, a motif as grand and humbling as the brilliant ponderous galaxy of stars. The past was no longer hidden, the future no longer uncertain, and the moment seemed to be a bright wisp of phosphorescent vapor, wandering over the landscape of time, or like a harpist's finger....I could hear the music of history being sung down in the black iron breast of the stove, in the white and tan and grey throat of the river stone chimney...the dark fire bubbling...the hushed smoke undressing its willowy body on the flat, white upside-down bed of the winter sky of 1868. The song became muffled; life once again began to hide from itself, partitioned in time by events.

"You know you're going to have to go back to wherever you came from, Paul. You sure can't stay here." It was the first time Charles had called me by name. His voice was low and a little ashamed. "I can't understand how you got here at all, not in the winter with no gear—no animal, nothing. There's no-place you could've come from less than two hundred miles from here. It's like you was dropped down right out of the sky, all clean, plenty of fat on your face. I don't understand it. I wouldn't be surprised if you was in some kind of trouble, but then that's none of my business, is it? Well, whatever your story is—and you don't seem any too anxious to tell it—you're going to have to move on." At the end of this little speech Charles lowered his eyes.

"I never meant to stay here," I said. "I never even meant to come here. As the matter of fact, this place wasn't even here."

"Now what do you mean by that?" Charles had looked up sharply.

"Alright, I'm going to tell you even though I know just what you're going to think when I get through. Although, I guess that's pretty much what you think already, so I guess it doesn't matter. So, let's just assume then, that I am, as you say, 'touched in the head.'" Charles and Irene looked at me with the open intensity of children. I took a cigarette from my pocket, opened the door of the stove, and lit the cigarette on a large orange coal.

"Anyway, what does being a lunatic have to do with appearing out of the sky—and I might as well have come from the sky as from Bingham, since there is no such town ...yet? The one does not explain the other, no matter what way you look at it. There is no normal way of explaining my presence in your cabin. It is a complete mystery...for me, too.

"I woke up at five o'clock this morning. The alarm woke me up. I spent half an hour trying to convince myself that there was something wrong with me, but I was fine, really—I felt fine. So, I had to lie, straight out—make something up that there was no basis for, at all. See, I didn't feel like going to work today; that's what I'm talking about. So, I called my boss on the phone—that's a thing you use to talk to people who are far away—and told him I thought I was coming down with the flu. Do you know what I'm talking about?"

"No, but go ahead," said Charles. His eyes were just slightly closed, as though he were carefully shading his thoughts. Irene watched me with bright intensity, her limbs poised, the green in her eyes, now, like the green that sometimes shines in a fall sunset. She said nothing.

"My boss had no reason to believe I was lying—I don't miss much work, as a rule—so he just said to stay in bed and take care of myself. I lay there for a little while, thinking, trying to decide what to do with this stolen day. Finally, I got up, dressed, ate breakfast, put on my coat and went outside. It was cold, but it wasn't snowing or raining, so I thought, "What the hell, it's a good day for a long walk," and I set off down the little highway that leads north out of town.

"I walked five miles to where the old door is—that's what's left of this cabin: the door, the foundation and the floor—and then stopped for a rest. I had planned to turn around here and head back to town. Actually, I don't live in Bingham but half-a-mile outside it in a little house next to the highway. But, of course it isn't there, yet, my house. So, I was standing by the road looking at the door. It was blowing open and closed in the wind. On the other side was just the forest and the cold sky. Then the door'd slam shut. Big old grey slab of wood. Then it'd fly open, again. I just stood there watching it, opening and closing as though a hundred people were going in and out of this cabin. A hundred ghosts. But, there was nothing there, nothing beyond this door. Just the cold, grey winter. And it'd bang shut and swing open, over and over—something that had gone on, and would go on, forever, it seemed. The land, the door, the land, the door, the land...a woman drying herself in front of the stove, and a man's voice: 'Aren't you going to close the door Irene? Close the goddamn door!' He suddenly appeared in the open doorway, grabbed the woman by the hair, and kicked the door closed. When it opened again it was just the frozen land, the icy little floor of a cabin long ago fallen down. Then it closed hard and I heard their voices muffled behind it. I walked over to the door to listen. When it opened again the voices stopped and there was, of course, nothing there but the low edge of the forest and a chilly little stretch of plain leading up to it. I went through the door and closed it behind me. At first I noticed that everything was much quieter; then it grew warmer, and gradually the light began to dim. And so I found myself standing in this cabin a hundred years before I was born, with two people who were long dead and probably forgotten...."

"That's some damned fairy story," grumbled Charles.

Irene sat straight and still, her eyes clear and wondering.

"How will you find your way home?" She asked.

"Well, I don't know how this works anymore than you do," I said. "The door opens and closes in the wind; it may not open on that stretch of road, on that time again for...who knows? A long time...maybe not ever. But, then again, it may be that all I have to do is open that door and close it behind me, and there'll be the road home." I paused and looked at Charles. Again, his face bore a stubborn and cruel cast. "Think of this, Charles, of what you yourself said: there is no place I could've come from, no way I could've gotten here. So, one explanation's as good as another. What's the difference if my story's true or not? Can you think of a more believable one?" I smiled ironically. Charles' eyes were hard black slots in his tough, weathered head. "Anyway, it doesn't matter. I'm going to leave....I'm going to try to leave, right now." I walked to the door and grasped the handle. Then turning back for an instant and looking at Charles on his big chair, and Irene on the end of the bed, next to the gun, I said goodbye and good luck and thanks for the coffee. Then I looked away, as though away from a dream, and turned the door handle.

"You murdering bastard!" Irene cried out suddenly, with piteous fury; and there was a shot as potent and decisive as the falling of the blade of death always is. It was as though my own mortality were a brass gong mounted in the center of my skull—a thing that until now had only occasionally been brushed or whispered against, once or twice lightly tapped by those events in life whose purpose seems to be to thrill one with the bright and fearful music of the infinite, to sound the grand trump of passage a hundred times before its *time*. But now the brass rang loud and finally as my mouth and nostrils tasted the acrid powder smoke that slowly choked the warm, homely air in the cabin. Again, I turned back to the room. Charles' hard, stubby body lay crookedly on the floor between the chair and the wall. There was a black and bloody hole in one side of his head, just above and forward from the ear; the other side was missing a fist-sized hunk. Irene sat on the bed panting; she laid the gun down gently on the flowered pattern of the heavy quilt. Her lips were parted and blanched and appeared to be speaking without Irene's knowing about it. A prayer so secret only the deepest loneliest part of her soul could hear and understand its own utterance. Then, her face softened. "He was about to kill you. He was going to shoot you in the back, damn him. I know his mind. I got to the gun first. Now I don't know what I'm going to do."

She looked at me with sad but harsh perplexity.

"I don't suppose you need to worry about the law, out here," I said with the far off voice of someone who is stunned, but has recovered enough to begin grappling with the practical matters of a catastrophe.

"No, the nearest law is on the other side of the mountains. They don't trouble with us. I just don't know what I'm going to do, that's all." Irene blinked and her eyes filled with tears.

There was an uneasy silence in which the question of Irene's future survival teetered haplessly. I looked down at Charles' body. That he had died in an aborted act of murder was reflected in the posture and countenance of his stiffening corpse. His face was a rigid mask of cruelty; the limbs were bent at hard and violent angles and, though lifeless, the once rugged body still effused a gnarled toughness. The hands and feet were twisted into brutal and inhuman shapes at the ends of the body, as in a final convulsive grasping at life. Charles was a sorry, rather than an awful man; he had been pounded harder and smaller and harder and smaller by the cold hammer of a life that was no friend to him. At the end Charles was a small, beady, dangerous man. There was little left in him of love or curiosity; killing and betrayal came easy, and death was no surprise. Irene was watching me. Her eyes flickered with a dim green dread. A fine shiver spread over her. Looking at her I realized that I was no longer a glib interloper from the next century who would vanish cleanly, having left no mark on the rugged surface of the past. Until now my sojourn had been merely a fantastic adventure the tale of which would probably remain a private thing, but which I would muse over for the rest of my life. Merely that. I would leave the denizens of this hour, this winter of 1868 to suffer their probably bitter, but already settled fortunes, while I would return by the same door through which I had entered, to my own time and season, back up the road to my small, warm house, just outside the presently non-existent town of Bingham. But now matters had changed, critically. Irene had saved my life and I had a certain duty to her. It was very hard, if not impossible, for anyone to make it alone on the frontier; and now, because of me, Irene would have only herself to rely on for the labor and substance of her survival in the lonely North American wilderness. Until now she had been somewhat more of an artifact than a real woman; now I had her life to think of, as well as my own. It was a grave and portentous situation, and I pondered it solemnly. Finally, I arrived at what I considered to be the right solution. I walked over to the wooden chair by the still belching iron stove, and sat down.

"I'm not going to leave you, Irene," I said in what was probably the most serious tone of voice I had ever used.

"It's an awful hard life," said Irene, evenly.

"I don't mean for us to stay here."

"Well, there's nowhere else to go. One place is as hard as another, in this country."

"There's a little house, Irene, about five miles from here—a house and a town with shops and people and a school and a library....And I have a good job repairing farm machinery, so you wouldn't have to do anything until you thought of something that you wanted to do. Just five miles to the south and a hundred and thirty years in the future—right out that door, Irene. Do you want to go?" I looked at her earnestly. Her face had turned round and soft and incredulous.

"You did have to come from somewhere, didn't you?" She asked, softly. "Bingham." She whispered the name to herself. "Do you think I'll get along alright?" There was an underlying firmness of decision to the tentativeness of her voice.

"People'll look you over. They probably won't know what to make of you, at first. But, Bingham's a friendly town for the most part, and if you stick around folks'll warm up to you. I've lived there all my life. I know everyone. So, that gives you one foot in the door, right away." I put my hands on my knees and leaned forward eagerly.

"They'll gossip, won't they," I could tell that Irene had made up her mind, "about me and you living together in your house." She looked resolute, already anticipating her indignation.

"Oh, they'll gossip. But, people gossip no matter what, anyway, you know that." I had already been the subject of many poignant and alarming tales that had circulated the barber shops, beauty salons, police station, tavern, the coffee shop and all the kitchen tables of Bingham. So, I wasn't afraid of one more go-round with the local scandal-mongers.

"You don't mind?" She spoke as if my disinterest represented a genuine sacrifice of some kind.

"No, I don't mind at all, Irene."

"Alright, I'll go." She sat very still, not even moving her eyes, looking at nothing. "I'm afraid, you know."

"I know."

"What should I take with me?"

"Not much."
"Will we bury Charles?"

Irene looked at the corpse for the first time. She seemed to study it with an artist's or a scientist's eye, without grief or remorse or triumph, but with the fascination of one who has discovered an unusual specimen or aesthetic subject and attempts to produce a clear and detailed mental figurement. If there were any sorrow or disgust—and those were there, yes, but only as the little wind of two dark feathers waving idly against Irene's impassive cheek—it was a general sorrow for all men who had been re-defined by vicious and inclement conditions as something far smaller and fundamentally less than men, and a general disgust for all the killed remains of such poor beasts. Having committed Charles' broken image to the blue memory of her soul, Irene slid forward on the bed, put her feet on the floor and stood up, decisively. She looked at me.

"Well, Paul?"

"Get your things together; I'll bury Charles."

"There's a pick-axe and a shovel behind the cabin."

I stood up, walked over to the corpse and took hold of the stiff, lifeless ankles. Irene opened the door for me, and with more effort that I would've imagined was necessary, I dragged Charles' body out into the sharp winter air, across the glittering, frozen ground. I could feel Irene watching me for a moment; then I heard the door close. I continued to pull the cadaver through the few knife-like slips of grey weeds and brittle clods when suddenly the cabin door swung open behind me with a bang, then slammed shut. I turned around thinking Irene had come out to help me, but there was no-one there. All I saw was the old door, splintered and pale from the hammering and tearing of the pitiless fists and fingers of hundreds of seasons passing, each trying to leave the whole world felled in its wake. There was no cabin; no Irene; before me was the familiar road; at my feet was a deadman, with an enormous bullet-hole in his head; a man who suddenly had no reason for being, or even a reason for having died alongside this asphalt highway, a few miles from a town he didn't believe in.

The car was just around a turn in the road, hidden by the trees. I ran for the door and pushed it open, but there were only the cold forest and flat, icy pane of the sky, glaring on the other side of the battered doorframe. I stepped over the threshold onto the broken little floor and closed the door behind me. Pressing my back against it, I stood panting and trembling, a sudden flush of wild listening as the hiss of the tires and the smooth, low rumble of the car's engine grew closer, emerging from the muffled cloister of the trees. The car slowed as it approached the clearing where Charles' body lay, and the old ruins stood. I heard the crunch of sticks and rocks as it pulled off the road. The driver turned off the engine and got out of the car. He walked a few yards and stopped. There was a dark silence, pierced only by the shrill wind.

"It's a body. A man. Shot through the head with something big; a .44."

Another man got out of the car and walked over to where the first man stood.

"He's a stranger for sure."

"We'd better just leave him right where he is," said the first man, "and go get the sheriff."

The two men walked back to the car and got in. The driver started up the engine, pulled back onto the highway, and took off fast toward Bingham. A tough lump of air boiled up out of my breast.

"Jesus, I've got to get the hell out of here," I said to myself, turning and grabbing the door handle. I yanked the door open and walked off toward the road.

"Where have you been?" It was Irene. She was standing up against the front wall of the cabin with a big bundle of blankets and clothing and pots and pans. Charles was gone; there were no tire tracks from the car that had just been there; there was no highway. The cabin stood, leaning a little to one side and a thin tangle of smoke rose from the stone chimney. "Well, which way is Bingham?" She asked, starting to pick up her bundle.

"I don't know," I said.

Behind us the door opened and closed in the wind.

LETTING THE HORSES GO

(FOR L)

Letting go is the hardest part.

We are in a village in Mexico, both in our seventies. You are leaving for good, I am staying behind. Scene with a horse drawn wagon, dusty canopy, dogs and naked children running, firecrackers and guitar music. You are in back, facing out, a sarape over your knees, waving. I am running with the children, throwing kisses, endearments, farewells. The wagon disappears around a bend, a cloud of red dust settles in the shimmering air. I give up the chase, stop, curling and uncurling my bare toes in the dirt, looking into the sky. Music, kids, barking, fireworks fall away behind me; you disappear from view, into your own future. I am left standing alone on a few spare inches of ground: the present.

Letting go is putting your hands at your sides, softening your focus. It does not mean pushing away, does not indicate loss. It means releasing your grasp on that which is in the sphere of your existence. When the horses are free to run they return to you with the wind. Vapors, lifted out of the sea by the heat of the sun, drift over the mountains, casting shadows in the forms of giraffes, human faces; a downpour bathes the earth, cold water washing into a valley, spilling into crevasses...and down, and down. Joining the great river, every whisper of the sea returns to her, singing together as one voice. If the sea was greedy and contained herself, grasping everything she touched, no rain would fall, no river would sing, no horses would be free. Letting go is breathing with the same force and surrender as the ocean.

Turning back to the village, I was surrounded by laughter and clattering bells; small, warm hands touched my clothes and skin. After a lifetime, you had gone off to look for something else, your wagon loaded down with cracked trunks. A smile extended further than the corners of my mouth, radiating all the heat in my body in a moment. The past whistled away among faraway peaks. We watched the clouds vanish over a white horizon; they were shaped like our faces. You, hanging your feet over the back of the wagon, me, hunkering in a field of grass as brittle and noisy as chopsticks.

Letting go is letting your love come and go; when it brings visitors, you are gracious enough to feed them. When the visitors wish to leave, you give them something to take with them, brush their coats and hold the door open. Birds fly in and out of the windows: if you close the shutters against them, you'll never hear them sing; if you put them in cages their songs will be songs of homesick captives.

A dry wind tickled my lips and eyelids. Insects scrambled off and disappeared back into the dirt. A boy brought me a fried cactus, a young woman sang under a tree, the melancholy of the guitar sweetened my blood, a tear fell on my cheek. Looking up, a cloud like a long silver letter opener raced across the sky. The earth made room for me, love settled over me, the cactus spilled open in my stomach, the grass became soft and wove itself in my hair and beard. Half asleep, I remembered your eyes and mouth, then, even the memory sailed away.

1988

Crying and Shitting at the Same Time

I HAD MY GUN AND I THREW MY GUN DOWN WITH REALLY A LOT OF ANGER AND I SAID HOW CAN A MOTHER SUFFER THE BIRTH YOU KNOW HAVE THE PAIN OF THE BIRTH TO HAVE A POLICEMAN AS A SON DYING AND GRIEVING PROCESS SO WE CAN USE THEM THE GOVERNMENT RUN RANGOON RADIO SAID COMPLEX YOU KNOW BELIEVING THERE ARE SOME AREAS IN BRAZIL THAT ARE NOT YET SURROUNDED AS TROOPS BATTLE WITH THOUSANDS I THINK THAT IT'S TRUE THAT A LOT OF PEOPLE I KNOW DON'T UNDERSTAND THE IDEA OF CONSEQUENCES THE WORLD OF PAIN AND YOU KNOW OF HAPPINESS MAKES YOU GROW NO MATTER IF YOU KILLED I'M GOING TO CUT IT UP WITH A PAIR OF SCISSORS THE MAN WITH THE SUNGLASSES GOT A CUP OF COFFEE AND CAME AND SAT WITH ME WE TALK ABOUT MANNERS I HAVE A REASON FOR DOING THIS OVER A TEN YEAR PERIOD MR. WISE FORMER AND CURRENT OFFICIALS OF THE AGENCY WOULD YOU LIKE TWO THOUSAND DOLLARS FOR JUST MAKING A FEW PHONE CALLS NOT LONG AGO I GOT A NICE LITTLE JAPANESE SHORT WAVE RECEIVER AND WHO HAS NOT HAD A TIN CAN OR A BOTTLE TO OPEN THIS GROUP URGED THE ADOPTION OF A NEW DEFINITION HIM THE WORD THE DIVINE SPOKESMAN THAT WONDERFUL MOMENT WHEN YOU FIRST HOLD YOUR DECISION THREE MEN AND A MAN PUSHING ANOTHER MAN IN A WHEELCHAIR ANOTHER MAN THE SAME AGE RUNNING A WOMAN THE SAME AGE HER HAIR IS FIXED SO SHE LOOKS VERY LIBERAL RESTAURANT WITH ARABIC WRITING EXPERIENCING BLOCKAGES ON YOUR

PROGRESS LOVE LIVING IN THE PRESENT LOOM AS A DIRECT RESULT OF YOUR CITY COUNCIL'S REFUSAL CUT BACK ITS TRADE SHOW BUDGET ABOUT FIFTEEN PERCENT WOMAN OLDER THAT THE THREE MEN WALKING WITH A MAN THE SAME AGE AS THE OTHERS A DRUG ENFORCEMENT ADMINISTRATION AGENT ASSIGNED TO INVESTIGATE A MEXICAN DRUG TRAFFICKING OPERATION THE TAPE PORTION ENDS WITH MR. LOPEZ A JUSTIFIABLE DEATH NEVER BRINGS UP PROBLEMS WE WERE BEHIND THE FEDERALS PANICKED AND HEADED BACK INTO THE INDUSTRY AND THEY DO NOT SEE THE SAME KIND OF SUPERNATURAL REALITY CROWDS OF AFRICA EXPRESSED SOME IN-SOTERIC SENSE OF CHANT OR BREATHE WHEELCHAIR DUTIES BECAUSE OF POOR PERFORMANCE SUCH A QUEST IS PROBABLY THE ULTIMATE THE WOMAN IS VERY SHORT THE MAN IS WEARING SUNGLASSES FOR THE BLOODY SUPPRESSION OF RIOTS IN MARCH AND JUNE MIST HANGIN' OFF THE END OF THE SEA UNDERNEATH THE WRONG POLITICS A GIRL CHOKING ON DRY CLOUDS OF HISTORY BASIC CULTURAL INFORMATION THE YEAR OF THE FUNDAMENTAL TRANSFORMATION GIVING POETRY READINGS SURVIVED BY HER SISTER TWO NIECES A NEPHEW FEEL THE HEARTBEAT MAYBE HE OR SHE LOOKS INSIDE MASCULINE WELL DEFINED FOCUSED PATIENCE OF VILLAGERS WOULD APPARENTLY NOT AFFECT PRISONERS SUCCESS COMES FROM A YOUNG MAN WITH SUNGLASSES WE CAN BRING A NO SPECIAL OCCASION GIFT YOUNG MAN WITH SUNGLASSES WALKING INTO THE RESTAURANT YOUNG MAN WITH A BOOK A PLOW STRUGGLING ALONG THERE GOES THE GARBAGE TRUCK AND A SPORTS CAR AND BIG LONG WHITE CAR AND A GOLD CAR A VERY SKINNY WOMAN SOMETHING IS MOVING BACKWARDS UNFREE SPEECH BY CALLING FOR NEGOTIATIONS GOT LIFTING A HARMONICA OVER A HUNGER LESS IMPORTANT OPENING AND CLOSING SEVEN FINGERED HANDS ONE COULD SAY THAT OKINAWA MORE THAN ANYPLACE ELSE IS HOME TO MANY SUFFERING SECRETARIES MILLIONS IN FADS WENT FROM SORTING CLOTHES AT THE SALVATION ARMY DEVASTATED POST-WAR MONEY

LOOKS AHEAD TO SEE THE MOVIES STILL GOING TO CZECHOSLOVAKIA POLAND OF THE WOMAN I LOVE THE TERRIBLE IRONY AS A GAUGE TO MEASURE SMOOTH NICE CONVERSATION BECAUSE A BIG PILE OF NEWSPAPERS FALLING OUT IN THE CONTINENTAL BANK OF ILLINOIS AS 1985 DAWNS AN INCREDIBLE AMOUNT OF NATIONS WERE TO FOLLOW SIMPLIFIED SKETCH PRESSURES ALSO REDOUBLED KNOW WHO HE IS AND WHAT HE IS LIKE THROUGH YOUR LACK OF ATTACHMENT THINGS HAVE NOT ALWAYS BEEN EASY FOR HER FOR THE FIRST TIME IN HISTORY POWER IN MUSHROOM FARMING INSTEAD THEY GET A BULLET IN THE BACK OF THE HEAD BUT SENATOR CLAIBORNE PELL BOILS DOWN TO WHERE WE ARE AND THAT'S A SERIES BASED ON FREE MONEY MAKING PLAN SKEPTICS ARE DOUBTFUL PEOPLE COULD GET KILLED THAT WAY STATE OF MIND YOU DIDN'T GET PICKED UP IN BRAZIL NOTICE IN THE SCRIPTURE QUOTED ABOVE MARRIAGE IS A PHYSICAL UNION PREPARATION FOR LIFE IT HAD SOME KIND OF DUAL MESSAGE WE DON'T HAVE THAT MUCH FURTHER TO GO THE CHIPPEWA RIVER AVERAGED MILLIONS OF BANKS CREATE MONEY INDEED THE SOURCE OF THIS FOREKNOWLEDGE TO THE RESCUE IF I WAS IN BRAZIL THEN USING THIS AS A TOOL TO CAUSE IMPACT YOU COULD QUICKLY RELIEVE THEM OF THE SUFFERINGS OF HELL HOWEVER MOVE YOUR LIFE IN THE DIRECTION YOU WANT TO GO THE MORE SO BECAUSE SUCH IMAGES MAKE ME FEEL ANGER OR HAPPINESS HAVE THE TOPOGRAPHICAL VIEW CENSORING WHO IN THE CAMPUS DEBATE CONDUCIVE TO THEIR RADICAL CONFLICT BETWEEN HUMANIST-BASED CRASH OF THE CONTENT OF THIS CONFLICT BETWEEN THE GREAT CRASH OF THE PEBBLES WHICH THE WAVES HAVE WRITTEN ABOUT OUR CRITICAL PROGRESSIVE EDUCATION HAS TAKEN US BACKWARD MASTER AND DISCIPLE CITY OF WORCHESTER BICENTENNIAL YOUTH RECEIVES RESOLUTIONS AMERICA UNGLUED APPROACH TO THAT IF I WAS IN BRAZIL A TYPE OF PANCHO VILLA OF NORTHEAST COLUMBUS YOU CAN START A REFORMATION OR BETTER STILL WE'D LIKE TO REMIND YOU THAT ADOLFO CALERO LEADER OF THE CONTRA FREEDOM FIGHTERS

HAVE NEVER RECOVERED FROM THE VIOLENCE OF BRAZIL MAKING A SATIRE MONEY MAKING PLAN SMALL CERAMIC VESSEL CALLED POT REGULARLY WITH OUR EXCESS MUCUS ONE FEELS LIGHTER OF TOXINS WHOSE MARRIAGE TO JOHN LENNON HAD BEEN BLAMED SUBJECT TO THE APPLICABLE RATE CARD MARIJUANA IN THE PAST MONTH AND ONE IN FIFTEEN DIFFERENCES IN THE WORDING WOULD BE RECONCILED CENSORING WHO IN THE CAMPUS DEBATE BASED ON FALSE TESTIMONY SOVIET CHRISTIANS ASK HOW PROGRESSIVE EDUCATION HAS TAKEN US BACKWARD PROGRESSIVES ARGUED YOU CAN START A REFORMATION READ THE BOOK WHICH CONTINUES TO INSIST THAT NO-ONE MOVE WITHOUT YOUR FORERUNNER IT WAS HOME AND THE HOUSES THIS VALUABLE BOOK WILL SHOW YOU WHY PROFIT IS IDEAS IN A POPCORN WORLD UPSIDE DOWN SELLING BOOKS BY MAIL BORN IN QUEBEC CITY, QUEBEC HE WAS AVALANCHED WITH POCKETS MORE JINGLE THAN FIFTEEN CENTS BATTLED HARD TIMES TO HIT BOTTOM WHEN YOU'RE DOWN ONLY WAY TO GO IS DOWN STOLEN LIFE MILLIONS IN FADS ABOUT THE BLACK EXPERIENCE OF PAINTERS AND SCULPTORS TRYING TO MOVE INTO THE MAIN PLATFORM AT WHICH THEY SELL THEIR CONCENTRATING ATTENTION AND YET A CIVIC SYMBOL OF NORMATIVE AND THERAPEUTIC PALESTINIAN YOUTHS KILLED IN THE WACKY TREND POLICE NARCOTICS DIVISION WOULD EXPAND ABOUT OUR SPIRITUAL PROGRESS FOR EXAMPLE BUILDINGS TO START A LOAD ALWAYS THE ADMONITION THAT THE WALKING OF A PATH WILL KILL YOU BEFORE JERRY RUBIN ALTHOUGH THE MINISTRY OF HIGHER EDUCATION IS STILL EMPHASIZED OVER PERSONAL MASTERY OF MOVIE POSTERS HOW CAN ANYONE BE A TIME THAT I WAS ON THE STAGE AND I HAD MY GUN REMOVED AT US THE WORLD OF PAIN AND HAPPINESS LIST THE EXACT NUMBER OF RELIGIOUS PRISONERS WIDESPREAD USE OF HALLUCINOGENS ALSO APPEARS IN ARTIFICIAL INTELLIGENCE NOTED THAT MOST U.S. STUDENTS DID NOT KNOW THAT COLUMBUS CAN PLAY A KEY ROLE IN STEMMING THE TIDE OF MORAL PLAYHOUSE WAS ROBBED OF THREE LARGE

CHANDELIERS NAMELY THAT IF SO MANY RULES ARE NEEDED GOLDEN PILLARS OF PROSPERITY FEEL EXACTLY AS PRESIDENT REAGAN IN THIS SCHEME OF THINGS REPRESENT MONOPOLISTIC POSSESSION BUT THE OUTWORKINGS INSTEAD OF KING ARTHUR, JOAN OF ARC OR GEORGE WASHINGTON WOULD CAUSE A TREMENDOUS IMPACT HAVE THE PAIN OF THE BIRTH TO HAVE A POLICEMAN UNGLUED CANNOT BE REGARDED AS AN INDIVIDUAL WHO CAME TO DOMINATE AMERICAN PUBLIC LIMOUSINE EMPIRE MUFFLER MAGNATE WAS WHOLESALING THE ROAD TO POOR OKLAHOMA SEND A BETTER LIFE FOR YOU PREPARED FOR SUCH A SUPERNORMAL IMAGE ROPE FALL IN TRANSFORMED GODDESS PERCEIVING DAY THAT MOUNTAIN IS LOCATED AWAKENS AND DOWN THE ROPE SELL PRODUCTS THAT PEOPLE ARE EAGER TO BUY AT PRICES THEY WANT TO PAY BECOME GOLDEN PILLARS OF PROSPERITY IT'S A SMALL GROUP PERCENTAGE WISE IN TEXAS WHICH HAS AN ESTIMATED 72 SLUGS WITH A PITCHFORK CAMERA IN HORROR EXPLANATION IS MEANINGFUL UNIVERSE THEN THERE WERE MY TEACHERS SWARMING OUT OF THE POLICE FOOTBALL THING MAKE PEOPLE LOOK GOOD SO THEY CAN GET JOBS WHICH CONSUME MY DELICATE NEGATIVE CONSCIOUSNESS STORM WILL SAY TO ITSELF THIS IS PREFERABLY INSIDE DEFENDANT ADMITS ROLE IN EXPERIENCING SUNSHINE WILL GO AWAY BEFORE WE CAN BE TRUTHFUL WITH OTHERS PANEL SET UP TO MONITOR THINKER OF OUR DAY AND A HIGHLY ACCLAIMED BABY STARTED TO HAPPEN YOU WISH UPON A STAR DISCOVERED THAT MANY EUROPEANS THUMBING NOSES AT THE INTERESTING DUETS HAVE SHOWN MR. LEWIS THE ANTEBELLUM SOUTH GOT A NICE LITTLE JAPANESE FROM MOSCOW CUBA AND MANAGUA HAVING A SELF-CRITICISM SESSION I'LL TELL THEM I'M HERE TO TALK ABOUT THE CONFIRMATION OF CABINET OFFICERS IN A NEW ERA YOU'LL ALSO LEARN ABOUT THE ONLY ALTERNATIVE TO A POWERFUL POPULIST FORCE BY CONCENTRATING ATTENTION ON NEGLECTED BLACK FIGURES A HAWK'S CRY HIGH ABOVE DEMOCRAT REPUBLICAN DIVISIONS TRANSLATED SIMPLY IT IS BEING TRUE TO YOURSELF ALONE THE SLEEPING GIANT WAKES.

His Last Hours

Man on a dirty cot, tube sticking out of his nose, open magazine on his chest.

"I've been useful all my life. Worked right up to the end."

"What do you want, Henry?" Another man sits with pen and notebook under a small light.

"Bury me in the junkyard. That's where I belong."

"You're a good man, Henry."

"Me and my old machine. Bury me with my machine."

"Okay. Is there anything you want now?"

"Beans and a can opener."

"No spoon?"

"And a spoon."

Henry ate the beans without sitting up, gurgling and spitting the red juice on his face and on the pillow. The other man switched off the light and sat in the dark. The shed only had one tiny window. The tube in Henry's nose hissed.

"How's the oxygen?"

"It's almost gone."

"Is there another tank?"

"No."

"What do you want me to do?"

"Nothing."

The two men waited, Henry coughing on a bean, the other man drawing and writing nonsense in his notebook. Henry deliberately swept the magazine off his chest onto the floor.

"That's the last thing I'll ever read."

"What is it?"

"*Digging Machine.*"

"Do you want to look at the equipment?"

"Get my oxygen."

Henry sat up in a painful jerk pivoting slowly on his hips and lowering his feet to the floor. The other man reached between the cot and the wall and lifted out the small green oxygen tank. He lifted Henry by one armpit. The two men walked to the low narrow door. Henry turned the knob and pulled. The two men walked out onto the hot gravel, the clear plastic tube swaying between them. In the distance were rows of digging machines, dump trucks, graters. One of the big earth movers suddenly started up filling Henry with a sad thrill.

"It's a good machine," he said. "The thing can chew the whole side out of a mountain in an afternoon."

"That's wonderful," said the other man.

"You know, I never had a piece of ass in my whole life, and I don't care." said Henry.

"The way these machines rumble and shake."

"You're a dedicated man."

"Let's walk on past the machines to the boneyard. I want to see the boneyard."

They struggled against the naked wind and the yellow dust toward the long row of battered and rusted machines. Henry's knees shook and the other man held him by the arm as they crossed the field of pitted gravel. A man sat high up on one of the earth movers working the throttle, shooting a black and silver jet of exhaust into the blue virgin sky. Henry and his old supervisor walked among the flanks of powerful equipment and came out onto a dry stretch of oil stained weeds. Beyond were acres of piled up wreckage. Not just earth movers but burnt-out cars, tangles of unidentifiable steel scrap, flattened and dismembered appliances, big bent up sheets of corrugated steel; all overgrown with vicious thorns and unhappy looking leaves. They wandered between the piles of weathered and broken machines and other refuse.

"I want to dig my own hole. Bring out my old machine and do it myself."

"Now?"

"Right now, while I can still do it."

Henry's machine was down at the end of the row, a tall orange gravedigger with a cracked rubber seat and dirty canvas hood on top. A steel ladder was bolted to the side of the machine. Underneath were enormous blades that could chew through stone and tree roots. Henry walked to the ladder, took the oxygen tank from the other man and climbed dizzily up to the seat.

He threw up the beans under the controls and sat down on the hot rubber.

"Are you alright, Henry?"

"The key's right where I left it. It's my baby."

And he started the thing, gunning the throttle and smiling, a bean stuck to the corner of his mouth. Throw the thing into gear and steer it out into the open. He turned the gravedigger around on its heavy treads and rolled over the weeds toward the vast overgrown boneyard pouring smoke and flecks of soot into the air. The other man followed with his hands in his pockets, looking up at the back of Henry's head, the little green tank sticking up over the back of the seat. Henry maneuvered the massive digger between stray auto bodies, wrecked cranes, dented and punctured sheets of steel. Finally he stopped near the back of the yard and turned on the blades. The other man caught up, puffing and wiping his bald pate with his sleeve.

"Is this it, Henry?"

"This is it," he half coughed, half yelled over the engine.

Henry lowered the blades into the hard yellow ground. The machine howled and screamed and sprayed dirt out the back. Henry breathed from his bottle and stared at the empty ground in front of him. This was where he had spent his life, up here working the handles, gouging out holes for the dead. He moved the machine carefully on its treads making the hole bigger and deeper.

"What are you doing up there?" asked the supervisor.

"It's got to be big, very big."

He worked the rest of the day digging a deep, shapeless pit. The other man sat on a rusted engine shading his face with his hand. Finally, Henry sat poised on the edge of the hole. He pulled the little tube out of his nose and tossed the oxygen bottle clanging into a pile of steering columns.

"Hey, your oxygen."

"It's empty."

"Get down off of there."

Henry rolled forward, catching his tread on the lip of the hole. The jittering machine toppled in sideways, Henry fell off the seat and was crushed under the flat plate steel side of the gravedigger. The thing stuck up over the top of the pit, the treads still going slowly round.

"It'll go 'til it runs out of gas, I guess," said the supervisor and turned and walked back toward the newer machinery.

Sissies Suck it Up (Bad Boys Gulp it Down)

These guys were very strange. They were into drinking piss—pissing right into each other's mouths, drinking the stuff out of bottles. I never understood them. They did it at night in the lavatory. It was like a cathedral in there. Thirty-six toilets—two of them worked; the other 34 toilets were full to the brim with the most horrible, stinking crap you can imagine. Just going in there was enough to make you gag, to puke your guts out. It was awful. At night, the lights were out in there. A dim, greenish light shined in through the high windows. Five or six men and boys stood and kneeled at the dark end of this room with their dicks out. No-one talked. There was a solemn, church-like atmosphere. You could hear piss splashing in throats, against teeth, on the tile floor; the sounds echoed in the huge, concrete lavatory. It would've been very stupid to be in there, uninvited. The dudes who were involved in this piss drinking thing were some of the roughest boys on the unit. Mess with them in any way, give them the idea that you think they're funny or fucked up; laugh at these guys and you are liable to find half your body parts floating in one of those dead toilets. These were no timid perverts, they were some real hard, crazy assholes. I used to stand by the door thinking, listening to the strange gargling noises, my mop leaned against the wall (I was the late night swamper) waiting for someone to say something. They should've been talking, degrading each other in there, that's what I thought. I waited for: "Drink my piss, sucker!" Something like that. Or: "Hey man, I'll give you five dollars if you let me unload in your face." But, there was nothing. They snuck in there silently, at night, did their business, and said nothing; then they went back to bed. One of them had a key to the door. I slept next to a piss drinker he smelled terrible.

One night I was in the big day room mopping, nothing going on between my ears—I was just staring down at the red linoleum and working my arms, that's all—when one of those bad boys came in with a quart plastic bottle. He walked over to me and unscrewed the top. "I'll give you a cigarette if you piss in here," he said in a low voice that was both menacing and seductive. He was completely straight-forward about it; he could've been asking me to make his bed, or give him my dessert. I wondered what this might mean, pissing in his bottle; what did it signify in their piss drinking religion when they hit you up for some piss? It could be a *very bad* thing. I was afraid. But, *not* giving it to them—that could be a lot worse. There was no way to tell. It might just mean that they were all dry. I looked, indirectly, at the man's blanched, sullen face. "Okay, sure," I said, trying to sound carefree. I did it right there in the middle of the room, under the flourescent lights. The pervert studied me hard. I took out my dick, held the plastic bottle up to it, and let go.

"How's that?" I asked hopefully.

"Is that all you got, boy?" He leaned in on me.

"Hey, I can't....You know....That's all there was....I was really squeezing...."

"You fucking sissy motherfucker."

"Do you want me to try some more?"

We both looked at the bottle.

"Fuck it, here's your cigarette."

He took the bottle, screwed the cap back on, gave me the cigarette, and walked off. I took out a match, struck it on the side of the bucket, lit the smoke and picked up my mop. A radio played behind the locked door of the office where the technicians hung out and bullshitted until six in the morning. They didn't hear anything in there. They never had any idea what went on on the unit, at night. People would get raped or cut up; no-one would know anything about it until morning. Then, everyone would say:

"Oh, what? Hey, I was asleep, man, all the way out. I didn't see a fucking thing, alright?"

Even the punk with the bloody asshole or the six inch gash in his face doesn't know what happened.

"It was dark. I couldn't see who it was."

The daytime technician would maybe make a short speech about raping and cutting. But, the technicians were as violent and twisted as the inmates. The little talks didn't mean shit.

I slopped the grey water around the big red floor, and thought about those bad men in the dark, back behind the toilets. It was a secret power ritual they were doing, using this urine, like a sacrament, to make themselves more than men. Drinking piss made them stronger, more brutal and depraved; it gave them an advantage over the other cranky motherfuckers in that place.

How did they recruit new men? Who was invited to join? Was this something that went on on the outside? I thought of men I knew on the street...hard men. I pictured them standing around in abandoned basements sucking on gummy glass jugs of old, old urine; laying face down in steaming pools of the stuff; down on their knees, on the cold damp cement, catching it hot from each other's half-hard cocks. I tried to imagine men I knew well doing that. Maybe....

I guess I am not a serious enough dude to get let in on this piss drinking thing.

Now, eating shit: that's what a punk would do—down on all fours, gobbling it up off the filthy tiles, sucking up black pools of diarrhea. Guzzling hot, salty piss is for very heavy males. I thought what a sissy I was: "Maybe I should eat some crap." Get all the punks and sissies together some night late....

What people eat vomit? Is there a different supper club, a secret lodge for connoisseurs of every bodily excretion? Snot...blood...bile...tears....It was hard to figure out. I was kind of a tear sucker. I felt for the men and boys who were getting raped over and over and over, night after night. The special favorites who didn't even moan anymore, but just gasped a little as it went in. And, then they would cry and cry, and I would lay awake, thinking of their tears, my throat stiff. So, there were reasons, things that happened in your life that made you hungry for something made by someone else's body.

I finished mopping the big room and leaned against the wall, waiting for the floor to dry. From the other end of the hall I could hear the piss drinker's voices, the whispers and gulping noises echoing in the enormous concrete and tile lavatory. An ordinary sound in this institution familiar and reassuring, like the wooden ticking of a grandfather clock in a big, empty house. And the crummy music and dull talk behind the heavy locked door of the office. The other madmen in *there*, with their huge salami arms and white buck shoes. I chewed a piece of gum. State gum, made in a penitentiary. "Tastes like a moth-ball." At the far ends of the halls were the dormitories.

The steel doors were locked until morning. I thought of the rapists and sadists in there working on their victims.

I couldn't hear anything. They were too far away, the doors were too thick. When the floor was dry I moved the chairs back—160 chairs. Then I started on the long, empty hall, slapping the mop against the office door, as I worked my way past it; I felt small and hollow, suddenly violently depressed, as I finished up the job. Miles of red linoleum, the color of dried blood.

The moproom was unlocked. I squeezed out the mop and put it in the corner, with the push broom. Then, I picked up the mop-bucket and emptied it into the sink. I set the bucket on the concrete, walked back out into the gloomy hallway, and closed the door.

They were still in there doing it. I crossed the hall to the lavatory door and listened. A dull voice said:

"Hey, Froggy, lemme have a taste of the swamper's stuff."

The man took a big swallow, choking and gagging. I could hear him struggling with his guts, in there. Finally, he got it to stay down.

"This dude's on some awful kind of drugs—that is some bad wee-wee."

"No," Froggy croaked, "He's a Jew. That's what Jew piss tastes like."

I went down to the office to get a technician to let me into my dormitory. A large, hairy man named Charles came out. We walked up toward the end of the hall. He held the key ring in his fist like brass knuckles.

He didn't look at me, or say anything, at all. When we got to the lavatory door, Charles stopped.

"You know what they're doing in there, Katz?" He asked firmly, looking straight ahead.

"No." I looked at his face; it was red like the linoleum, like jellied blood.

"I do." We walked the rest of the way to the dormitory without talking. He let me in and locked the door behind me. I walked to my bunk, sat down, and took my shoes and socks off. Then, I got under the blanket. I lay there and listened. I was thirsty for something.

Woman With One Eye Open

Look at me you sonofabitch, look at me. I'm giving him the eye, what the hell's the matter with him? To hell with him. He's good looking, but he's dense. Like most men—dense. To hell with men.

I'm working on an afghan. Light blue and coral. I'm going to put it over the back of the sofa. I'm making the afghan to brighten up the apartment.

I hate this guy. He won't look at me, the sonofabitch. I'm giving him the eye, but he won't look at me.

I feel like a devil. My hair, my jacket, everything. I'm out to get a man, to get him in my power, to hypnotize him. I feel slippery, evil.

I've been living in the same apartment for two years. There are pictures on all the walls, I hate bare walls. Everything smells like sandalwood—I burn incense all the time, especially in the bedroom.

I'm from Arizona. I came here because of a man. Because I was mistreated. Because I was tired of Arizona. Everything there reminded me of the man. So, I had to get out of there.

This is nothing like where I come from. Except the men—the men are the same.

Look at me. Turn your head. You are under my power.

My life is getting better.

I've got my eye on you.

The Tour

One way to control people is to keep them hungry and on the run. A long tour with a sketchy itinerary, poor accommodations, hectic schedule, scanty diet. Keep the people moving. Give them a hundred things to do. Make them identify and explain themselves at every turn. This can be seen as a way of life. One is preoccupied by hunger, does not have time to consider where they are going. Everybody laughs. The tour has an avowed purpose. People tumbling, scrambling over each other to get there first, to get at the food. At the same time, they are being drilled, driven along, pelted with contradictory instructions; they are broken up into groups and given jobs to do. There is one compulsory gala event after the other. They have to struggle for even a small moment in which to catch their breath. The tour is a drill; the drill is theater. It's a way of life. No-one knows whether to take the intent of the tour seriously, or not. But, as long as the players go through the motions of the production, it doesn't matter. The way of life is a success; the tour is a success.

Drill masters are drilled by other drill masters, rushed panting and hollering slogans from one place to another. Everyone has a sense of their own importance. Everyone is always in question, and is made to answer for themselves, over and over. There is a seat of power, and there is an illusion that there is someone sitting in the seat of power, directing the tour, the drill, the lives of the tourists. The seat of power is made up. A tourist is pushed into the seat—he sits there waving his arms and screaming. The Grand Drill Master.

The tour grinds on. People imagine they are going home. When they arrive at the place they think of as being home, new demands are made of them. They are moved from one end of town to the other, from one room to the next. Voices scream at them through closed doors. There is a constant pounding, a beat to which they find themselves running, working, talking, making love.

The crowded trains are leaving. Loud voices on the platform calling out destinations, instructions. No-one is sure what they are hearing, anymore. Everyone moves toward the open doors of the train, crowding together, trying to get in. The doors close; the train goes screaming out of the station. Another train pulls in, comes to a halt. A fevered, hungry mob disembarks.

1986

VISIT

I saw you through the window trying out the furniture. You went from one chair to another carrying a plate of cookies and a teacup. Finally, you sat on a green armchair and put the plate and the teacup on a small oval table. I went to another window and watched from behind a bush as you ate some of the cookies and sipped the tea. There was an open magazine on the floor at your feet: *Mending Broken Bones*. You looked at the pictures as you ate. I walked around the house to the front door and knocked. You answered the door wearing a different dress.

"Would you like to come in?"

"Sure."

We walked to the room with the chairs. You sat on the green chair and I sat on a straight blond chair.

"Would you like a cookie?" You held out a cookie.

"Thank you." I took the cookie from your fingers and put it in my mouth.

"Would you like some tea?"

"Thank you."

You left the room through a low narrow door. I looked at the pictures in the magazine as I chewed the cookie. You returned through the little door carrying a steaming teacup.

"Here is your tea."

"Thank you." I took the cup from your fingers and filled my mouth with tea. You were wearing a different dress.

"I noticed you're reading about broken bones."

"Do you like them, too?"

"Yes."

You turned the page with the toe of your shoe.

"Here is a broken hand. The whole hand is broken."

I swallowed the cookie and tea. The damage was caused by a tomato-peeling machine. You read the paragraph out loud. Your naked voice aroused my own throat.

"What will they do with the skin?"

"I don't know."

"Where is the toilet?"

"Through that door."

I went through the door and down a hall. The bathroom was at the end of the hall. I opened the door, went in, and closed the door behind me. Then I threw up in the toilet. After flushing the toilet and rinsing out my mouth, I went back to the room with the chairs and sat down in the straight blond chair. You sat in another chair, wearing a different dress.

"Do you feel better?"

"As much as I like broken bones the pictures make me sick."

"Not me." You turned the page with your toe. A shattered spine.

"It says here there are nine breaks. This woman is dead." You looked up. Your eyes were like Vaseline. I avoided looking at the pictures. Instead, I looked at your mouth.

"Then, there is no point in mending those bones."

"They did it anyway."

"Please put your feet over the picture."

You covered the magazine with your shoes.

"Does it really bother you?"

"Just right now." I looked at your blue shoes.

"Thank you, Helen."

"My name is Beatrice."

"Thank you."

Suddenly, you moved your feet to one side exposing the picture of the broken back. I gagged, but continued to smile.

"You can throw up in your teacup if you want to."

"Thank you." I held the teacup to my mouth but nothing came out.

"That's funny."

"I'll show you another picture."

"Okay."

The next one was of a crushed head. I threw up on the small maroon rug.

Woman with Blond Hair, Eagle Face

I have a disease. You can't see it. My doctor can't see it. I am very angry—I want you to know that. I am angry at you and I'm angry at my doctor. I am being killed by my disease and you—you and my doctor—are standing by, doing nothing. You smile, you say "Of course, of course," but you are humoring me, you don't believe me. I don't have long to live. Think about it. My whole life has been a long ordeal. Coddling a useless husband, rearing two selfish and brutal sons, and before that: my father was a strict disciplinarian—I learned to take a serious lashing without a whimper. My mother died when I was five. I was molested by my older brother. What do you care? It has not been an easy life, no. Now I am dying and no-one feels it but me. Now you think I am full of self-pity. Well...I am alone and I know it. When I die....I know how to take a whipping. Nothing will change, everything will just freeze—my eyes, my mouth, my thoughts.

I walk through the crowd. Everyone is laughing and eating. It all looks far away, it's all behind me. These young men with their beards, and their shirts open; the women with their breasts free, their lips parted. Everyone is looking for sex. I don't blame them. Get it while you can. It's too late for me—I'm all withered up. I'm too sick for sex. It won't be long. It'll all be over. No-one will know what it was. A disease no one could see...that no one believed in. Not you, not my doctor, not anyone. I'm too old for sex, too old for this young living. It's too late.

JUNK

Car hoods, bathroom tiles, clock faces, walls peel away in layers and collapse in the streets. Broken water pipes spray. Cracks in the street open their lips and show us the insides of their dark mouths. Fires spit and smoke. The air shimmers in the heat. Everything has been rearranged by the bombing. It is all junk, fragmented and dislocated; the meanings of things altered in a second. Everything has been reduced to the same status: a grandfather clock, a burning tire. Things to step over and around, to get away from. Bodies dumped from their windows onto the sidewalk—it's the same—take the rings and money. Later, everything displayed in a museum as treasures, historical relics. A fingernail, a shoe, a brick. Everything further disoriented, made even more useless by isolating it behind glass where it cannot be touched and will have no further use. I see my eyeglasses in there, my typewriter and pens and hats. Artifacts. The meanings of these things have become rigid. When life stops the lives of the objects that surround it stop, too. I pray for someone to break the glass and take my typewriter, look at the world backwards through my glasses. Or give everything back to the weeds and the weather. Let the rain trickle through the bombed out city as the black rubbish is swallowed by tree roots. Let the bones lay where they are.

And make the artists caretakers of the worlds, leftovers. Assign them the job of returning life to the vanquished. By putting a flattened toaster on the wall, it still has its little moment. Let them see everything differently and transform the ruins by changing our perception. After the big one: the planet as a dead philosophic puff-ball. We will remember things before they are gone, see things before they appear.

The sky is already heavy with bombs. I envision them turning around, falling away from the earth, space junk diminishing in the distant blackness. Maybe this vision will save us. Picture of a war inverted, clamoring to un-fight itself. Build an enemy for it out of its own waste.

I want to drive the car with no wheels, pray the broken rosary, arms with 20 faceless watches. Line up all the odd paraphernalia and study the work of man. And when the bombs come crawling down the sky, we will work our bodies into their casings and talk sense to them, having learned their language. All the clock dials shattered, the time of attack never comes.

The generations of throwaways as unconscious offerings to a salve for the desperation that created and discarded them. Human bones and tools and weapons. The trappings of belief. Junkyards and mausoleums squinting under the sudden arc-light of interpretation. The eye searching for a key in the immense dumps of civilizations, obscure systems of mechanics, inscrutable religions. History screwed around and splashed hilariously in our dawning windows.

There is the whistling, decaying junk of our bodies. Shall we nail our own limbs to the gallery walls to change the perceived meaning of humanness? I offer both arms and legs; my head in a fish tank slick with green algae. I fight a war with myself in private and deliver up the remains. My personal effects are piled in the middle of the floor; torso bound with wire, dangling from the ceiling. I am now the mute property of intellectual fashion, open to mob scrutiny. On exhibit: the collected refuse of a life. Everything has become valuable. Buyers leave with toothbrushes, discolored organs, dictionaries, eyes.

Still, the richest junkpile is the broken body of a war. A continent turned to an artifact of conflict. I invite the missiles to aim themselves at my skull. I declare myself a small but dangerous country. Slivers shoot from my pores. I await your reply to my death warrant. Nothing has changed since the last war. Girls play in a wrecked fighter plane; canopy dusty and shattered, weeds grow in the controls, piss smell. Why change anything? I invite you to pick through my ruins, wander over my bombed planet.

Finally, the art, too, and all the excited revelations are refuse, exploded by war, carried off in canopied green trucks and dumped in thorny canyons. A clear rain washed away the ashes. The faces of rusted appliances like baked flesh under the sun. Men stand on the edges, eyes blurred by the heat and confusion of constant wrecking, throw in their watches, boots and uniforms, dive into the thorns and rubbish, each man experiencing personal planetary destruction. Perception dying here, overcome by vegetation and insects. The last truckload is in. Whispering of the girls in their airplane.

SISTERS

I said then she said then I said then she said. That's how our conversations always go. We get off the phone with someone else, then we call each other up and tell each other what we said. We've been doing that for, God I don't know, ten, fifteen years—somewhere in there. That's all we do. There isn't even any phony little chitchat. Nothing. And you know there certainly isn't any....We definitely never discuss anything real. All we talk about on the phone is what we talk about on the phone. And we never talk in person, we only talk on the phone. You know I am not such a shallow individual. There are things I'd like to be able to talk about with someone—with her. I've known her longer than I've known just about anyone. I wish I could talk to her directly. But, the only way I can tell her anything is tell someone else, then call her and tell her what I told them. Then she wants to know what they said, what I said back, what they said then, and so on. She never says anything about what I said, herself; she never asks me what I really think about anything. But then I'm the same way, huh? I guess we're pretty good friends, after all. Sisters. But, there's a deep side to me, a side that has thoughts about things, a side that wants to communicate besides on the phone, about something besides...she's gonna be calling me any minute. I'm gonna tell her what I just told you. Maybe we'll find some other way to communicate besides....I gotta get off the phone.

Plague Doctor

Here I am in a plague-stricken Mid-eastern city. People in hip-waders are combing the ancient sewers looking for rats. Rats are the key to knocking out the bubonic plague. I'm not really a doctor, but there aren't enough real doctors to go around. At least I can relieve people's anxiety. Already I have been the receptacle for two dozen people's last words. I feel very emotional.

Everywhere windows are shuttered against the heat. I am whispering as I drag my feet in the dust. Every now and then a car cuts around me; I hear the drivers cursing as though I am an ox. Fuck you too! Up yours! I don't budge one degree; I stay right on course. I keep walking till the heat gets me, then I enter the first door I see. The rooms are dark and damp and hot. The stench is terrible. All sorts of flying insects fill the air. The electricity's out.

"I'm Dr. English. How many dead have you? Are there any not yet infected? There's no sense lying about it."

Outside are flat-bed trucks carting away the dead by the ton.

We haul out a couple of bodies. These will be fed into an enormous bonfire a mile out of town. A hygienic precaution. The drivers are haggard, spectral. Their job is almost certain suicide. This is proof that people will do anything. How were these men recruited? What is motivating them?

I am wearing a badge I found on a corpse next to the highway. Dr. John English. I have his papers, too. But no-one's asking. They need all the doctors they can get—even bogus doctors. What could anyone possibly have to gain pretending to be a doctor in a plague-stricken city? This is more proof that people will do anything.

Soon there will be no-one left but a few weak doctors and the truck drivers. Then it's likely that these too will die. The city will be still...cleaned out. All the efforts to save a few people will have come to nothing, or near nothing. There will be a few who are simply immune...myself...a few others. Playing holy, running around being merciful. The drivers will start dying as soon as their job is done—it's the insect mentality. They will have pulled through this far by marching blindly through disaster. I will be sitting on a high wall. Thousands of rats will be floating belly-up under the city. I can hear some of them still squealing, through the storm drain openings. A pall of silence is spreading over the city. The screams of the dying are fewer. Only the wind and far off, the ocean...a few hushed voices. Everything seems far away.

I'm looking at a pocket-watch. More scavenging from the dead. Why not? All their relatives are dead too. So, I lift a little something here, a little something there. What's the difference? The watch reads 4:43. Afternoon. Soon I'll go looking for something to eat. I'm not afraid of being poisoned—I'll eat the first thing I find. Oh, I'll probably sniff it first; make sure it's not too old. Then I'll eat it. It's a cheap pocket-watch, but what the hell? It ticks...I imagine it keeps time. I saw a couple of pounds of coffee earlier today. I wonder if the people in that room are dead yet. I can't remember which door it was. It was on this street, I remember that. It's almost evening. The dying slows down at night, just like anything else. It rests, it sleeps. The sky is growing quieter, deeper. Sounds all seem like they're coming from farther and farther away. Clouds pass overhead like great big gloved hands; their shadows float down the street, over walls and rooftops. As the afternoon grows darker, I smoke more. I have plenty of cigarettes; that's one thing I brought with me. The smoke rises into the dry branches of an olive tree.

A cat walks in the shadow of the wall that delineates the town. He is undisturbed by the quiet. When he gets to me he weaves his path between my feet as though they were rooted to the ground. He, too, is an observer. He is not concerned with the outcome of the tragedy, yet he is aware of the suffering and death around him. He hears the rats squealing in the subterranean water-ways but wisely he avoids them. Instead he feasts on birds and large insects. The cat stops and seems to contemplate as bodies are carried hand and foot and on stretchers from the dark doors of the buildings that line the street. The cat is a priest in the same way that I'm a doctor. He bestows his blessings calmly. Beethoven piano music ends abruptly—it had been pouring from behind one of the shuttered windows. In the silence after the music we hear gasping and crying; in this city of either dead or not-dead, those are healthy sounds. The cat stops ten feet away, turns around and looks up at me. We recognize each other mutely, as outsiders. Surely we are both immune. We are, in a very real sense, bandits, highwaymen. We are also holy, healers. We both wound up here from faraway by simply shrugging at the news of the disaster, and continuing.

Let me recite a list: shoes and socks, notebook, stethoscope, doctor bag, jacket, pens, watch, hat (my size), four gold rings. I found these by the roadside on my way into the city. Now I carry them around and my arms and legs seem too long. It must be obvious that all I have is stolen. I feel so clumsy. So, now I'm confessing. If you can't forgive me, at least you've heard my confession.

Father Cat feels no guilt. He hears my mumblings of pain and purrs. "It is nothing, my son." I wonder if it's wrong to laugh at all this dying and suffering, to take it too lightly. On the other hand I am trying to help. I have gone from house to house calming people down, reassuring the dying and the families of the dead and near-dead. Now the cat accompanies me everywhere. He advises me on moral issues. Everyone wants to keep the cat—he keeps their attention off the plague. Also they imagine he will kill rats. He's too smart for most people. Not that I'm so smart; but my connection with the cat is casual.

One of the wagon men realizes the hopelessness of his job, his part in the drama of the annihilation of the city. He leans against the truck and weeps. His brown skin is soggy with sweat.

"Here, let my give you a shot. I have some medicine that will help you." I opened the bag and took out an ampule of methadrine and a hypodermic. A few moments later the man was sailing. I tossed the empty ampule and used syringe in the street. The cat ran after them. As a quack I favor the use of powerful drugs, things with very definite, pronounced effects. People mistake that kind of effect for magic, and the one administering the drug for a wizard. They're a lot less likely to ask questions when you've got them bombed out of their minds. And anyway, the wagon man needed some actual magic to penetrate the dense spell of so many cadavers, of the fire, of the disease.

Beethoven again. Anything to block out one's own moaning. The music leads right back into the present reality and hence starts sounding more and more like whimpering. But one no longer recognizes the pain in their own voices. And Beethoven is certainly not the best example, not in my opinion, anyway. Mozart is probably the most powerful of the narcotic composers...the classical ones. Music is very helpful when people are dying. It's something to focus on as life is receding and the tunnels around one's vision are growing blacker. The music is wonderfully dramatic. Even the cat is moved by it.

"He has died! This time he has died!" This is a woman's voice, the powerful voice of a large woman. It's coming from the same place as the music. She doesn't bother to turn off the music. It continues to play, now in the background. Finally she opens the door and steps out into the street. The wagon men approach her wearily.

"Doctor! Doctor! Why didn't you come and do something? Now he's dead."

"A lot of people are dying. I'm sorry."

"AHHHH. AHHHHHHH." She begins wailing. Me and the cat look at her, blinking. The two wagon men walk around and past her, into the dark room. "No, no! Don't touch him! Don't take him away!" She runs into the room after them. There's a certain amount of scuffling and crying. The wagon men come out carrying a man's body, followed by the stricken woman. They put the man's body on top of a pile of corpses in the back of the truck. The woman cries and cries, she stands in the street crying. Finally she goes back into the room with Beethoven; she joins her weeping with the music. I follow her with the intention of offering her drugs.

"Let me give you a shot...something to calm you down, to ease your suffering."

"No, I don't want anything. I don't want to turn into a drug addict."

"It's your choice."

The woman stops crying audibly, but the tears continue to run down her cheeks.

"Oh, go away. Just go away."

"Can't I stay and listen to the music?"

"Alright. I don't know what I want anymore, anyway."

"Thank you." I sit down on a beige ottoman and lean back in the dark, against the damp plaster. The walls of all the buildings, every room, are sweating in the heat. The music does not act as a balm, it drives me deeper and deeper into the catastrophe. I think of fighting against it, or of going back out into the street. Somehow this stance—troubled by Beethoven, sharing the air with this stranger's grief—is really correct and above-board. I can't, in fact, shift my position. The air is heavy, blue-dark. The woman's large body shakes under the cloth of her dress. I can see the lumps of fat on either side of her knees quivering. This real, and final kind of sadness is so clumsy. Every attempt to keep one's composure only makes it worse. This woman shakes with grief, but doesn't utter a single peep. Idly, I wonder where she is getting the electricity to run the record player.

"Where do you get the electricity for the record player?"

"Batteries. Under the table. *His* batteries. *His* record. *His* record player." She looks up at me and suddenly straightens her shoulders. She wipes back the wet strings of green-black hair from her forehead.

"Now they are my things. I will listen to the music...even when the electricity's out. It goes out often here. He got the batteries so he could always listen to music. He listened to the music until he was dead...he listened and I listened with him. All you could think of was to give me a drug...a shot. Hahaha."

"You'd feel better. It'd make it easier." I believe what I'm saying is true.

"Maybe easier, but not better. The music makes it better."

The cat settles on the ground between her feet. He looks at me, he looks up at her, he looks across the room at a black doorway, he closes his eyes, responding to the doorway with a darkness of his own. I think of my two cats at home, in America. I think of my record player and my records. The electricity has gone out twice in my life—once for half an hour and once for ten minutes—I don't worry about it happening again.

Outside the truck starts up, its doors slam shut and it drives off. I can hear the heat from its exhaust pipe crinkling the air behind it—I can hear it, or maybe I imagine I can hear it. Now there is no-one standing in the shade of the olives tree across the strip of dust, the street outside. The patch of shade is a bit of comfort wasted in a city where suffering is rampant. Like my bag of drugs. I think of the truck and its two men parked on some other street waiting for the dead and waiting to die, themselves. Every now and then what they are doing, what they're involved with, catches up to one of them—his knees buckle under him, he cries and sweats. Finally, both men continue. Elsewhere in the city there are more like them.

The Beethoven comes to an end. She puts on music by an Italian composer I have never heard of. This music is lovely, but it's complex, hard to listen to. Strings and woodwinds. When I'm an old man I'll understand this music. The woman sits on the edge of her tired bed and folds her fingers in her lap.

"You don't like this music."

"No, I like it, but I'm confused by it."

"The composer is Italian. He lived to be a very old man."

She straightens her dress. "Aside from your work as a doctor, what do you do?"

"I am a spy."

"For what country?"

"Oh, just as a hobby...for my own satisfaction. I like to know what's going on under the surface. It's very expensive. I travel all over the world."

"I've lived in this city all my life. My husband was an American. He stayed here after the war. He was too tired to go home. He used to be a musician. I never heard him play, and he rarely talked about playing music. But he listened to music all the time. Fine Music. He taught me all about music."

"Then he left you something. He didn't leave you with nothing."

"No. And there was a little money, too. Enough to live on. I'm only being realistic."

"We shouldn't talk so much."

"We should listen to the music."

There is no more dying on this street. Most of the rooms are empty. Outside, through the storm drains one can hear the mad chase going on under the city. But on this block the dead are all dead and the living are few and mostly silent. The heat shivers in doorways, uncertain whether to cross the thresholds. The record player dances with a cheerful waltz—it sounds insane to me, in this setting. The cat walks over and hops up in my lap. He's drooling cool saliva against my shirt. I am afraid he may be sick.

Then I think of the woman. I wonder if she's sick. It never occurs to me that I might be sick—it simply isn't possible.

The cat doesn't die. The woman lives for years and years. I return to America and am perplexed, absorbed by my memories of this and other travels.

Early 1980s

OUT OF THE PICTURE

This is not a maudlin or romantic decision. I only want to see myself as removed from the picture of crunching bones.

Now, I am in the faded bungalow. The garden is disorganized. Dirty bottles lined up on the stoop. Laying on my side on the yellow grass, I un-read the news. The events of the day are driven back into themselves, and simply do not happen. This done, I go back to pruning a dying bush. It is very hot here. 103, 104 degrees. The bottles are from drinking water. A truck comes, but I am not here; the man takes away the empty bottles and leaves fresh water. I find my pen in the dirt, under the bush. I think of going in, out of the heat and writing something. It would have to be something that could not be remembered, or even understood. I can no longer write about things that contribute to the collective disorder of human thoughts—but, I cannot help writing such things, either. It is the long knife edge. I pick up the pen and continue working on the bush, wiping my face with my hat. Tough, purple-grey flowers fight the awful heat, their petals clattering like dry toothpicks in a sudden breeze. I know I am where I belong: you can no longer see me. I am not on the map. Everything I touch disappears. I only have my little sphere. I drink my water and work in the garden. Go to the stoop and pick up one of the bottles; drink an inch of warm water. There are bugs in the water.

No-one has seen me buying groceries. They take my money and their eyes see birds and clocks—they dream, momentarily. Make no impression, there is no memory of me. I have an old car. The seats are dusty and the rubber mats on the floor are piled with bones and desert weeds. The engine makes a dry, puffing noise as I drive on the white highway with my food. The windows are down, my glasses are blurry with sweat. Turn off the highway onto a straight, sandy road. I can see the Spanish bungalow six miles away. Take the road at 110, skid to a stop, raising a cloud of harsh, yellow dust. The bushes are still. The newspaper lays in a position of death on the grass. There is no hope for this grass. I see myself, having assumed a life of solitude and invisibility, as contributing nothing, as privately undoing history.

But, it's not possible. I realized that one day while killing ants in the kitchen. It reminded me of something. The common murderousness. The banal and unseen acts that cannot be undone. I watched the hundreds of ants, stunned by the poison, struggling in the dark plumbing. On the table were two pads of yellow legal paper. I turned from the scene of death—I had no feeling—and sat on one of the chairs, at the table. The pen was lost. I watched the paper, saw different things writing themselves on the lines: expressions of my desire to grow smaller, other confessions. I wrote with the ink in my eyes, read and erased the words, forgot what I had written. I grew more and more insubstantial. I went behind the house and fired my shotgun into the blind desert, over and over, killing nothing, aiming at nothing. Then, I walked back into the house, laid the gun on the table, over the yellow paper with its unwritten words, went out the front, crossed the small dry yard, got into the car, and started it. I leaned on the hot steering wheel, thinking, with the engine running.

There was an enormous pure white rock, a boulder with a flat, sloping face, 20 miles south, hunkering in the sand, next to the highway. This was my image of the world...smooth, reduced to silence. I liked to sit by it, feeling simple and transient as the dust, denuded of consequence, a papery man pressed onto his own spare vision. Looking through the windshield, the unpaved road disappeared into rocks and weeds. The bungalow stood, unremembered, near the end, chewed on by sand and insects. You cannot see me here; no map maker can place me on the earth.

I turned the car around and drove to the highway. Miles are uncountable in the desert. Distance is a trick. Time slips by unevenly, marked by erosion. The rock was as clean and hard as ice. The rest of the world seemed dim and confused, dumped haphazardly at the foot of the magnificent boulder. I drove the car off the highway, onto the sand, rolled to a stop in the uncorrupted shadow of the rock and killed the engine. Sensation of hurtling into a vortex where all ideas of a photogenic, image-rich reality are dismantled by the emergence of an ironed-out anti-history of the universe. As one departs, even the word "goodbye" is absorbed. Memory is truncated, severed parts abandoned, replaced by unintelligible whispers of the secret imagination. A bald lizard, twitching in the heat blinks one eye, and disappears in the sand. The far-off mountains look like rows of teeth; the desert glows pink...soft, oral flesh. I have found the bright gullet, the little slide where the known swallows itself. For me, this is the center of hope. I am not a pessimist—simply, the thing has gone on too long as pictorially isolated from, and therefore in rabid conflict with itself. Ethnicity, language...a systemic dishwater. Knowledge is always in violation of itself these days. Our collected images simmer in a bloated sump; it becomes impossible to reconcile our visions. Everything is blurred—my glasses, the windshield, the sky—all rushing into itself at one point. I am first to go. I opened the door, got out of the car, climbed the rock, lay face down, arms and legs spread out, loose. I waited for the rock to close around me. A clean chill bit into the desert. The top of the sky was the black of closed lips. A thin river of my blood wandered on the mountain ridges. Finally, the cold and dark were absolute. I imagined myself sinking into a stomach, my substance drawn away, used to feed the bodies of the stars. I had fled from the picture, and could conceive nothing, myself. The car door swung closed. My back was damp. I stood up on the rock and looked into the cold, blind air.

Faraway, a fire burned. It was shaped like an ear, and it shivered against the glassy black of the sky. "Twenty miles north," I thought. Impossible to tell in the desert. I slid down off the boulder, walked to the car, opened the car door and got in.

Yellow pads and shotgun curled up in smoke. Bottles shattering in the heat. Lost ballpoint on the dashboard. Bushes and hard flowers seared into a spray of brittle ash. Grass withered to oily black. House on fire. History wringing its hands in the sky in huge, slow gestures. The mop of smoke. I drove back up the highway through the dirty windshield, red thumbs pressing against the closed lip of the night. Turning in at the narrow, unpaved road, I drove to the bungalow and stopped the car. Windows spilling flames. The garden lit up at night. Brutal shadows. I got out of the car and walked to the smoldering lawn, face lit by a small model of the sun. Newspaper spitting yellow ashes. That night I slept on the front seat of the car, in the dimming light of the fire, the small picture of which I had been a part, now much smaller.

In the morning I drank water from the radiator, then drove toward the town, 40 miles away. I stopped at a filling station for gas, oil, cold pop. The man at the pump said: "Was that your house that burned down?" He looked right at me. "Now I am marked, again," I thought. The man whose house burned down. Once more coupled to an event, to the endless freight train of events. Speeding out of the desert, away from its town and its still smoldering pile of ashes. The white rock shining under the new morning sun. There is no way of disassociating. Our doings and machinations, everything is slip-locked into a jittery montage—the banal and the fantastic—for perpetual replay. The thing feeds on itself. "Yes, that was my house." I paid the man and turned onto the interstate.

1989

Tired

I'm tired. I've been through so much. And, when I think of the future....Even when I was a little girl, I'd think about what I was going to do when I grew up and I'd feel tired. So, it's not like I went through some trauma and now it's getting to me. I've always felt this way—I've felt this way as long as I can remember. I was one of those kids with a premature long face. People would look at me and feel sad. When I was seventeen, eighteen, and I was going out with boys, they were always a little too considerate; they treated me as though my whole family had just been burned up in a fire. Everyone was always trying to figure out what was the matter. If they asked me I'd say, "Nothing, I'm just tired." And, that'd be the truth, but no-one ever believed me. So, I'd let them think what they wanted. Now, no-one asks. You know why? Because I don't look sad anymore, I don't look rundown or cranky, I look menacing—I look like if I got my hands on a gun I'd put a few people away. Maybe it's true. Maybe I would. You know why Doberman pinschers are so edgy? They are born with a chronic migraine headache—their brains are too small for the inside of their heads. So, they feel pain from the time they are born, from the time they are able to feel pain. I was born tired. The world, life, everything is a big conspiracy to keep me awake. I'm getting really irritated, really angry. Look out, just look out. I wish you all....I wish all this would just go away. I'm so tired.

Daily Erotica

These days it is mostly jacking off. I do not get laid often. I have vivid and compelling relationships with the women in my fantasies: there is always a romantic angle, or else a distinctly (and pleasantly) unromantic angle—sex with strangers or enemies—but usually I like the love affair. I can hear the bodies moving: mouth, vagina, prick, skin against skin, zippers, shoes, hot breath coming from noses and mouths at the same time, filling burning armpits, cracks of asses, little confused choking sounds. All of this begins to smell to me, too, very aquatic, like a warm green sea on the very edge of a dark, mouldering jungle with huge coral flowers with bright yellow and orange stamens, mad brilliant green trees swarming with monkeys...growing right down to the sand, webs of dry seaweed, huge pink conches, smooth slices of mother-of-pearl. No, no I am not thinking that this would be a good place to fuck—I do not like to fuck in the sand. But it has always smelled this way to me, shrill rotting seedbed singing into the mouth of the sea. It's some memory, I bet: when I was little, 5 or 6, I had a girlfriend—we were married, in fact—and we used to go back into this swamp that ran right up to the ocean—cattails, snakes, ferns, huge iridescent beetles, drooping yellow trees, slimy green water with big frogs and lily pads....The fresh smell of the sea mixed with the thick, rank smell of the swamp....We'd crawl in among the lilies, take off our shorts and touch each other's smooth, undeveloped genitals. I must use the word "blissful" though I feel it is a dilapidated word—it reminds me of faded loveseats with broken springs, and spiritual con games. But sticking my dirty little finger in Kathy's jinee, surrounded by high fragrant foliage, frog noises, crowings, rustling, and the strange mingled fresh-sour wind, her small mud and leaf-stained hand cupped over my hairless, very sensitive little scrotum...the air filled, as I see it, with the excruciating (raw, naked) smells our bodies would later learn to produce on their own. The kind earth lent us her sex smells for our first pleasure. I have to use the word "blissful" when I recollect this thrilling, so affectionate, thoroughly simple lovemaking.

All this comes back to me every time, transformed. The sea, swamp, the jungle flowers, dying rotting, giving birth and being born. It's not the same as when I was 5—the whole earth is new and I myself have been reborn and rearranged so many times—but there is still the thread that runs through all the twists and breaks and dawnings and horrors and soft afternoons spread out on the bed under the hot blue window. Alone dreaming. Used to be somebody there. Once in awhile somebody there. Now anyone I want. But they always leave so soon, I can't hang onto them, they just evaporate. Now, the radio, you know, that's where I turn next. I go right from this fantasy I can't sustain—from a damp shoulder rolled across my throat, mouth against my ear—to Dr. Walter Martin, The Bible Answer Man, as I fold up the little piece of paper with the semen on it. All the no-good pages get torn in half and put in the nightstand for this purpose. I think it is a good use for bad writing—jacking off on this failed typewriting somehow redeems its failed intent. The room cools down very quickly and turns brown. The radio voice drones and cackles. I put on some tea and go to the typewriter. The woman comes back and there is a gust of salt-fish smelling wind. She says she has good news for me....I can't hear the rest. All I can see is her shoulder: it's brown and full and there are goosebumps. I'm writing a letter to a publisher in Cambridge, Massachusetts. "I have some good news for you, Jesse...." There is one breast showing—the woman's breast is covered with goosebumps and the nipple is drawn together tight as though she's just been swimming. I don't always know who I'm dreaming of. Bible Answer Man is a call-in show. Voice on the radio says, "I prayed to Jesus and I promised if I got through to The Bible Answer Man I'd send the IRS what I owed them." "I have good news for you...." I couldn't finish the letter. I sat on the bed smoking and listening to the radio.

The longer I am alone—I mean unattached—the more involved my fantasy life becomes. Once I didn't have sex with anyone for two years. There was a picture of a naked woman that I had cut out of a magazine—a very plain picture—that I carried with me everywhere, folded up in my wallet. The woman was short and chunky and had black hair. At first I would just take this picture out, look at it, jack off, fold it up and put it back in my wallet. It was very convenient; I could do it anywhere—I'd be in the middle of a meal in a restaurant and get up and go to the men's room; or in the waiting room at the doctor's office I'd go to the receptionist...."I have to go to the toilet." After months or weeks or something of looking at that woman—her body, her face, trying to see what was behind her model's expression—I began to have some friendly, and even romantic feelings for her. Of course in reality she could've been...who knows who she was in reality? But the woman I was looking at was learning to play the cello and convinced me to go to concerts, and when the concerts were over I would always head straight for the men's room. But sometimes now, I would just take the picture out and look at it and put away. I went to four concerts in a row of Mozart string quartets. I listened to the music with a special attentiveness because of this woman whose thoughts were in my heart. After the last concert I rushed home—my face and eyeballs and ears and cock were full of blood—ran up the stairs to my room, went in, locked the door behind me, got undressed, lay down on the bed and turned on the reading lamp. I reached over, took the wallet out of my pants, pulled out the little picture and laid it next to me on the bed. I laid on my side with my arms out as though I were holding someone; I wrapped one leg over the top of "her" legs. I looked at the picture a long time, then, slowly, without ever looking away, I closed my eyes. I felt someone there with me, a friend, her body. It was impossible...it wouldn't have made sense for me to masturbate. I didn't want to move, at all, or open my eyes. We talked and kissed and I fell asleep.

We, the two of us (I can't bring myself to type out her name) took ocean voyages on old and exotic wooden ships to countries I have never heard of. She became a great cellist, and she would practice as I sat at the typewriter, or worked on my enormous paintings. We didn't talk, in the usual sense, but I felt that we communed in a way that was meaningful. It was very much like being in love. I was so hard up, you know...this thing had gotten out of hand. One day a friend came over with a big jug of wine; we drank it out of quart jars. Drunk and raging around the room I told him all about my affair. I said I was in love, I described her to him. I hummed some of her music—she composed a lot of music—but when I got to the voyages, some of them years long...to countries he had never heard of....So, okay! I offered to show him a picture of her, the only picture. And I got out my wallet. I had been carrying that picture around for a year-and-a-half folded up. Very carefully I took the picture out and peeled it open.

"That's her," I said.

It was falling apart along the creases and I had to hold it very gently with both hands. The paper was thin and rough and the corners were worn away. My friend leaned over, squinting; he looked at the thing like a diamond appraiser. Then he raised his head and looked at me the same way: "There's nothing on that paper, Bernstein, nothing at all. There's no picture there." I looked down at my hands and cried.

Not long after that horrible parting I met a short woman with red hair who immediately—and I mean immediately—drove me to the ocean. We got to this dark beach at one o'clock in the morning and we sat out a long and wild storm in her van. We fucked on a little mattress in the back. When we got done we both said: "Well, now that's out of the way," and we relaxed and talked together until long after the sun had come up, and the storm passed. Then, we made love. She was my lover and best friend for four years.

We took a lot of trips to the ocean, and we lived together on two different islands and in some very peculiar little towns. We went to a lot of classical concerts together, and she introduced me to many of my favorite authors. Very suddenly and mysteriously she shunned me and all her other friends and went to Oxford, England with a Rhodes Scholar. No reason, no quarrel, nothing. "There's no picture there." Another parting like the sudden shriek of a falling tree. The fantasy did not reflect itself on my life. And I wasn't looking for someone to replace the lover I had created, and lost, to be her. But the two types of experience do bleed together in startling ways. Every lover I have had has seemed to be a figure from a mythology I had forgotten and was on this earth to be reminded of, rejoined with—a mythology that has yet to be realized, that must be remembered at the same time as it occurs, in order to become part of the past, to become myth. This vanishes into the dark, scatters among the stars, and shines down on us forever. Influences the shape of things, the pool of dreams, the odd fate of the living, forever.

The steamy bodies who people my fantasies walk through glass doors, stop on the sidewalk in front of me. I stop, they turn but do not look at me, walk to the corner and wait for the light, cross the street and are gone. Later that day they return naked without their shopping bags and umbrellas and they are so much softer. And a few times it has gone almost just like that for me. The intangible myth is as real as the desire that conceives it, draws it shimmering into the harsh matrix of everyday life. Our dreams settle gracefully into the haywire truss of our tangled-up needs and struggles, and softly speaking to us wait for us to realize them.

My dreamboat
Lands with no names
Miles of hot black sand
No, I don't want to fuck in the sand
I want to fuck sand
Her voice
a warm cello
a thousand breasts
with nipples like
large brown eyes
returning to sleep
our bellies touching
our knees
groins and toes touching;
our shoulders and fingers
our faces touching.

"I have good news, Jesse," she says into my mouth. "We're going home soon." The dreamboat's sails open and close like hands, palms to the wind, glorious in the sun. And we roll on the sea—the blue and green and brown; the every color sea—to a land whose name I will not remember until I arrive. But, I have visited her many times before. She tells me that it's home, and I know it is. The fluid language, the dank salty air, the people whose bodies are whispers, the humid jungle growing right down to the sea. The whole thing is a kiss. The whole thing is touching our adult bodies. The whole thing is finding our way in and around, navigating our bodies that are nameless lands, that are each other's homes. Home.

Sex is one way to go home. Like playing the cello inside someone else...laying their most secret music with your hands...discovering that you are the naked instrument filled with your lover's music painting your giant paintings of man figures falling into blazing red. "There's nothing there. There's no picture." Just the mainline. Frosty vapors coagulate into flesh and love visions who start to speak and vanish hissing, my solitary passion escaped through a puncture in the weak wall of half-rotted need. Imagination slices itself up desperate to reconstruct its own body. Burnt waffle face, plastic vagina funnel, smell of gasoline, no arms, no hands at all—big red alarm bells plugging up the raw stumps. My dick lays there small and cold, half sheet of no good typewriting in my wet hand, pants around my knees. The room is filled with sunlight. No home. No home alone. Home alone she sits across from me: "Hon, most don't even have pelvises; just look at the way they walk; it's as though their legs are screwed right into their guts." The red hose rolled up in the garage, in the dark, in the back in the mouse droppings and brown motor oil, drowsy odor of old rubber and stale lawn water. Dad's useless penis. Except when it's time to crowd up the house some more. My friend with his full brown body covered with goosebumps, sucking each other's dicks in there, under the boiling black roof, behind mountains of wet newspaper and rusted and broken patio furniture. Smell of gasoline. His cock tastes like shampoo. We love each other, but we're both waiting for the girls. A pink plastic funnel. This untroubled sex drains out fast. Soon our lives will depend on a part of us we have lost contact with, our legs stuffed up into our ribcages. The rest locked in the garage rubbing up against the dirty walls. How do you get in there? How do you get that out of there? Just the mainline. The whiff of salt and dripping succulents that kill me back to life. The wet vagina behind my own balls. Dreamboat. I am the only woman I can dream about, but I can pretend she's anyone I want. Moans, throat clasping itself, one half word. Listening with an ear between my shoulder blades—a big protuberance made of red muscle. The china rattles. One cannot wait for love—the earthquake is coming. It can be done in pantomime, as easy as mowing a lawn. Acting on instructions from the heart and sex desire, printed on the spinal cord with pointed silver nerve riddles, with aimless shards of lightning from beyond the-homely blue hem of the sky—the last bright slivers a trillion light years dead and collapsed dust. The myths fly from the ends of darkness and infinity and settle in our bodies, fill us with dread and desire, make our sex smolder and flare, our hearts pump many things besides red scientific blood, imaginations try and create living flesh, nameless lands and ships that could never sail...and I lay on my bed and touch the part of myself that is supposed to be special. Not this time—no picture. Mainline full of sweating foxglove. "Now I look ridiculous. I didn't even do it." Pants up fast. Do the zipper and belt. Put the bad writing back in the nightstand. Smoke. 22 tea bags.

These days it's mostly a wish. But wishing's okay for awhile.

UNTITLED

There was a star over the water but Maurice turned his back on it. It shone on his wet hair and on his wet, pink, rayon shirt. He took a black plastic comb out of his pocket and held it up in front of his eyes. "I am an animal in a cage. I can't escape." He was a big, impassioned man, always panting and sweating and licking his lips. He wiped his forehead with his bare forearm. "The trees are disappearing, moving farther and farther away." He moved the comb back and forth in front of his eyes. "I'm pacing back and forth in my cage." He swayed back and forth. Maurice was standing up in a rowboat, drifting away from an empty beach, late at night.

He had been at a party at one of the big, expensive houses just beyond the row of trees that lined the water. Everything had tantalized him—the women, the exotic garden, the cars parked out front...other men's things. He ate and drank a bit and took off walking, down to the water. Maurice stood on the beach, looking around. There was an old skiff leaned up against the bank. He could see it in the dark, its shape blacker than black. Up above, between the trees he could see the peaked roofs of the big houses, big luxury liners. He sat down in the cold, heavy sand. "I'll take that little boat and get the hell out of here."

Maurice took hold of the skiff. It was wet and weighed plenty. He dragged it slowly across the beach to the water. Then he got behind it and pushed it in. He got his shoes and socks and the cuffs of his pants wet. Looking up, Maurice saw the star. He hopped into the boat and turned around, so he was facing the beach, the bank, the trees and the row of great houses. He could hear the party over the lapping of the water. Slowly, as he drifted out into the bay, the sounds of expensive cars coming and going, of light, chirping laughter in the garden, sunk into the darkness beyond the trees. The star lit up the silver ribbon of beach. There was a man out there waving his arms. Maurice sat down and waited.

Several hours later he awoke in bright morning sunlight. He was all the way at the other end of the bay, drifting toward the city. Like any other immigrant, he checked his pockets for money and identification. $14 and his driver's license; he was okay. Maurice sat down and relaxed; there was nothing he could do but drift...drift and wait. The sun burned off the last trailing wisps of morning fog. It was a warm, breezy day. Maurice thought of his car parked all the way at the other end of the bay, and this little boat—somebody else's boat—there was nothing, really, that he could do with it, but just set it adrift again, once he reached the city. There was no rope to tie it up with. He worried about these things for awhile, and then he set to dreaming. He dreamed of the party; of the tables of food and liquor, of all the pretty and friendly people....

Finally, Maurice had drifted close enough to the wharves that he could make out fish stalls and sailors and shoppers and baby buggies...whatnot. A few fishing boats and tugs were tied to the pilings. Maurice drifted toward the forest of fat, creosoted pilings. Here and there a ladder hung down to the water. He was glad of that; he had wondered how he was going to get up to street level. The skiff bumped into first one piling and then another. He grabbed ahold of the sticky wood and pushed off toward one of the ladders. It took him a few tries, but he made it, at last. Maurice climbed up the ladder and onto the wharf. He could hear the little boat rattling around lost and empty, down below. Nothing he could do about that, no. He walked up into the city, as if for the first time.

After having eaten a huge breakfast—steak and eggs and toast and potatoes and waffles and fruit and cereal and juice and coffee—Maurice went to one of the waterfront bars and ordered a Boilermaker to warm himself up with. He'd been out on the water all night in a flimsy shirt, with soaking wet feet. His bones were cold. He sat down at the end of the bar for the rest of the morning and all afternoon until, finally, he was out of money. There was nothing left for a tip. The bartender stared at him as he walked out into the darkening street. Maurice took off walking toward home. He lived on the other side of town, so it was going to be a long walk. That he was a bit drunk made the prospect of walking all the way home at night less gloomy.

Up one side of a hill and down the other, then up another hill and down the other side of that one. Turn a corner and down a hill, then turn again and climb another hill. Maurice walked long into the night. Finally he began to recognize the streets. He was back in familiar territory, maybe half an hour's walk from home. He stopped at a bus stop on a dark street and sat down on the bench. He was no longer a zoo animal. He leaned back on the bench and let his head flop all the way back. His neck was tired. He had his eyes closed. Suddenly he opened his eyes and looked around the sky. Tonight there was no star. Maurice stood up and looked ahead of him, up the sidewalk. Once again, he found himself adrift. Home was always somewhere else, over there, and there was never any assurance that it would be there at all, when he got there. He moved aimlessly across the cold cement.

A Serious Crime

It is a crime alright
a serious crime
according to the law
the law that is always changing
there are new changes everyday
the blank anemic law
a riddle of sterile conflict:
according to this law
it is a crime,
yes.

There is no way I could've taken him to a hospital. They would've sewed him up and handed him over to immigration. Immigration would send him back where he came from. The cops down there, when they got their hands on him, would torture and kill him. If he broke under torture they'd track down his family—everyone he knew—and they'd get the same. So, taking him to a hospital or calling a doctor...it was out of the question.

He was hit in the lower abdomen by a shotgun blast fired from a range of eight to twelve feet. Cutaneous, subcutaneous and abdominal muscle tissues were all severely damaged. Major portions of both upper and lower intestinal tracts were perforated by birdshot. Sections had to be removed. The interior abdominal wall was not seriously damaged.

The attack was apparently an attempted murder; it could also have been a robbery aborted when the assailant realized that there was another occupant in the apartment. I lived three doors down the hall and went—immediately upon hearing the gunshot—to the apartment where the attack took place. The only people in the building at the time of the shooting were the victim, the victim's roommate, and myself. No-one had called the police. The victim's roommate urged me to help, but explained that the man could not be taken to a hospital or treated by a licensed physician.

I treated the man for shock and performed a preliminary examination of the wound. Then I left the building and went by car to a medical-dental building. I entered by a basement window and went through the building taking whatever supplies and equipment I thought I might need. I returned to the apartment with these supplies and attempted to apply appropriate surgical procedures. Much of this was improvised, since I am not a trained surgeon. My training is for emergency pre-treatment and stabilization care in combat situations. This does not include diagnostic or procedural technique for culminative correction of a severe injury or condition. However, the treatment was apparently effective, since the man developed no major infection(s), is now able to take a liquid diet, and, while he has some neuropathic symptoms, these seem to be due to normal trauma related to the injury, subsequent treatment, and circumstantial stress. I think the man will survive if the law doesn't get him.

1986

THE HARBOR

The long neck of the harbor clogged with broken and derelict scows, refuse. The air is darker and more odoriferous as it approaches the flabby body of land. Men wander with dirt in their eyes, not having bathed for years, eyes red with undefined passion. Women lay ruined among boards and cracked rubber. Here and there a small fire burns and smoke rises, soft as forgetfulness. A train grazes the spooky inland hills. Faces and trunks orange in the shadowy windows. Further inland there is nothing—blackened trees and yellow dirt. But, somewhere there is another sea. Everyone struggles towards it, as though all their dreams are hiding under its surface.

A man uses himself for bait, tied to an enormous steel hook. The black hemp digs into his abdomen. "Going for the big one," he hollers, lowering himself into the slippery water. A boy watches him go under, as he pees in a can. Then, he turns and faces what's left of the sun. *The big one.* Green and solid a decayed copper ingot rising and falling in the old brown muscle of the sky. He heaves the can against the water, as into a blind mirror. There is nothing under there to capture. Strangers are everywhere, powerful and dangerous. Men with sharp, poisonous nails under their clothing limp along, vending treacherous versions of the truth. Women follow them, blinking as though hypnotized, holding strangled animals in the air, their starved arms quivering. Dust rises from the stone quarries and temples at the end of the land. Picking at a cluster of pimples and scabs, the boy follows the mob.

Out there in the west everything is done at once. Gods are yanked from the heavens, stones are dragged from the earth, commandments are uttered, sacrifices are slaughtered, blessings are received, everything is forgotten, distorted. An atmosphere of decay blows down the infected throat of the harbor. Children shovel mud for handfuls of anything anyone will call food. Appealing and passionate songs rise from small holes in the sticky earth. Musical instruments hover in the air. *The big one* flops onto the slick and filthy deck of an appalling ship and vanishes nightmarishly over the long burning line of the horizon. Lifeless dust and fire in the west.

The can bobs in a yellow circle. All the gods at once are called into the air because of an endless desperation, called to the altars of their oily temples whose hinges and gates collapse, even as the mouths of the supplicants squeeze out their wormlike prayers. The man suffers on his hook, beneath the surface. Imagine! He is looking for the strange image of the sun down there, as though it was a deadly fish. And, the boy stands on a small hill watching the beginnings and ends of several quizzical phantoms of belief in the distance, on the long rosy peninsula.

Looking down into the pit of a carved out animal scrambling with slaves and priests and their mumbling sycophants. Smoke and swaying splintered scaffolding. Bloody mops. The naked form of the beast revealed by torchlight. An animal goddess fitted heavily into the grey meat of the promontory closest to the dancing black ocean. Men drooling with idiot faith, tossing their offspring into the pit over the dusty heads of the slaves, as though this would give life to the mad creature of heaven. A sudden wind blurring the slack eyes of those who were already falling out of faith, selling the stones of the pit—for anything, a bite of nervous skin, peek into a yellow eye crawling with lice. Boy watching from a lifeless bare rise in the dirt, penis dribbling, scabs drawing together, eyes clear as melting ice, looking down into the fevered belief of man as it is shaped at the edge of this devastated harbor by the light of orange and smoky fires, by both willing and unwilling hands. Looking down into a staggering relief of feet, belly, clawed hands...ferocious lips.

Bitten off steel hook rising from the sloshing water, bait snatched, a pool of bloody urine. No *big one* down there. His eyes look burning into heaven. He thinks of the inland train, passengers sinking into sexual acts as a last resort, having ceased to believe in another ocean, in their submerged dreams, a destination more compelling than the journey, itself. The manacled and stitched body, chewed in half, at the bottom. A forgotten wad of sopping flesh and filthy intestinal ooze. The boy imagines, for a moment, that this memory will save him. Then, his imagination shifts to the green platform of sun on a swift and distant ship, surrounded by the brutal stamping feet of foreign sailors, a toothless and limping captain, captured bodies tied to stakes, still wiggling. The deck is awash with blood and spit. The sun knows nothing of the goddess into whose empty body it will shine. Slaves fall screaming from the scaffolding. An enormous fish with deteriorated lips and no eyes leaps howling from the putrid harbor and lands helpless on a field of smoking tires. A flash of burning oil. Eyes suddenly appear in a roaring cloud and settle on a flaming skeleton. If the alert and dangerous eyes of the priests had seen it, this accident would be the seat of a ruinous belief. A blind woman warms herself in the stench.

There is a clash of steel. A war has broken out in the distance. Bodies fly in the darkness. Maybe the train will be stopped at one of the ever-shifting borders. Wet dicks will go limp. Vaginal tissue will turn dry and stiff. Assholes will shit and mouths will start jittering in an attempt to speak, to excuse the slobbering of the body. Everyone will be harnessed and made to pull. Great hunks of the earth will be hitched to the train. All the fleeing passengers tethered to an unceasing chain of messiahs and gods, goddesses and dripping wounds. The prophets will fall upon them with whips and slashing teeth. Not a kind word will be spoken. When skin touches itself it sounds like panels of metal, grating and banging. The terrible water of the harbor rushes in and captors and captives gasp, struggling to escape, drowning, climbing over one another, no longer sure who is bound.

A scene of endless war, tearful faith and brutality. Words of passion are pronounced, drifting up from grates imbedded in the yellow dust, turn to restless gurgling in the flood from the west. Some imagine that the ocean is reaching out to clasp itself. Others say the waters steam with revenge. Those who are bent on destroying meaning dunk their heads and suck, as though sucking fire. Their abandoned clothes float, smoldering on the surface, like slag in a quivering furnace.

After the civilizations. Or, when civilizations rise and are destroyed and forgotten in a few seconds, the slaves who build and tear them down rising in whistling jets of steam. Nothing is remembered. The shoreline keeps shifting. Borders shake like whips, breaking the back of the world, chasing the little people up and down the valleys. Poets wail. The sunsets are so greasy. Again, the prophets ferocious. The boy thinks of moving to the edge, getting away from all this deadly activity. He hobbles along on sore feet, trying to remember his mother. He is attacked by a community of beggars who drain the water from his blisters, proclaiming that it is pure. He lets them suck his scratched body. *They will evaporate.* He thinks. The war dies down and shining towers appear in the north, out of reach. One sees the lights of the promised city and is filled with a ripping hunger, like a furious machete in the guts. Then the city vanishes screaming, the mottled dream of an infant. Another crusade, an empire, and again, it is over.

The boy reaches a low bamboo fence. A luxuriously fat woman tosses around dirty and naked on a little square of fragrant grass and flowers. She waves a medallion at him, lifts her belly. Her breasts are yellow and overgrown with moss. "Mako!" She says. From then on the boy thinks of himself as Mako. He is unable to forget her huge buttocks as he wanders along the fence.

1989

A Likely Story

The sun comes up like a spent penny. Losers will be losers. Oh, it's windy on the bridge, and blues play in the fingerprint eyes. Checked it for signals and it doesn't remember the game. Shotgun in the groin. Baby-proofed. Burnt liver and pants. Taste of blacked out potatoes. No sign of work. Everything caved in around the shoulders like a collapsed building. Just the word "mother" and a dead battery. Never shaved. Scorched denim color iris. The big blue and red sign still lit up—it looks so pretty against the sky. A cloud like a silver letter opener. I got my own tears, my own troubles. Carpet needs a shampoo, etc. My family is dying one after the other. Broken music in left fingers. Rotating pelvis as water spills out. Nothing more. Into the sack and zip it. The van disappears among the many black streets. A piano at a stoplight. They play all night, or they start pretty damn early. Bus stops filling with the mad and the hopefuls—none of these have a chance, you can be sure. It is not my job to predict. When people turn to trash I sweep them up and take them to the dump. How'm I to judge that? Everyone looks so ratty. The president on TV looks like a pimp. Everyone looks like they are about to murder someone. That's how it looks to me. All the faces, they are lit from inside, they glow like jack-o-lanterns. So eerie. Terrifying. A pinball machine...bells, music, steel balls rolling everywhere. Replay! Replay! Tilt! Tilt!

The car rolls down into the parking garage. I do the report and go home. A door closes behind me. Everything seen through cellophane. The furniture like meat. The color of meat. Why did I buy furniture that color? Lettuce drapery. The place is white bread with mayonnaise. A sandwich. Wrapped in cellophane. I feel like a cockroach or a rat. Eyes bulging, little gnawing teeth. Bite through the glitz, the wrapper, get to the business. I am a tired man. I don't even drink. For me, drinking is like trying to inflate a slab of pavement, something very heavy with no more holes in it. Everything just runs off into the gutter. I have never puked on this carpet, but it looks like it has been puked on. And, it smells. It smells like oranges and catsup and sour cream. Like I throw my food on the floor and step on it. Just leave it there. Well, I can't shampoo the carpet, now. Fuck it. Lay down on the sofa. It's too big, the sofa. Big and square. Made of luncheon loaf. It stinks. That's why I smoke so much; so everything will smell the same. It's hard to find enough things in common from one moment, one place, to the next, to be sure it's all one planet. Ah, everyone's got some excuse. Something that needs an excuse. I'm just nervous, okay? Fuck you. Now I can't sleep. The sun looks green.

What is it about bridges? Blow off your genitals and jump. What does that mean? Many people get that same idea. I think it is a pun: fuck off. But, it is not a funny pun. It is not meant to be funny. This is a pun for someone who really wants to get in the last word, who has never had the last word. It is the end of a conversation they are having inside themselves. "Fuck off," they say. And, in their mind, nobody says anything after that. But, maybe on the way down, as they are bleeding to death and drowning: "Sit on it, punk." Well, it's an expensive statement, and does it come across? I've seen it over and over, the same thing.

Eat the sun. Little wall with it. I am laying on the sofa in my coat hungry, like this is a bus station. It's my apartment. I hate it here. All the florid memories of people's opened up kidneys, brains like cactuses. My reports read like a naturalist's diary. I have got beyond the whodunit stage of police work, beyond crime and solving crime. I look at people like plants. Plants strangle each other as a matter of course, and no-one is offended. Unless it is a weed. But, who decides what is a weed? To me it's all the same. Someone shoots a politician, politician kills and rapes a four year old. The garden is overgrown. Everything's sense of its own importance is bloated. It's just people claiming the ground on which other people stand, buildings crawling over each other to get in the sun. I swear, I am learning to live off the smoky light in the room. No, I am not much interested in chasing people around.

But, I do it. People pay me to chase other people, and I do it. Or to go out in a boat and pull someone up out of the water and make up a story about what happened—I do it. It is my job to make sure people do not have to think about these things. But, they think about it, all the same. People lose their appetites, can't sleep, go crazy and kill, thinking about it. I am hired so people will know I am there, and that's all. And, I go from one stained room to another. People cry, beg me to make it stop, and I promise to do what I can. Which I do. Which is nothing. I am a paid witness. I have seen. I see.

One up, one down. Two down. The other one up, and the other down. These are games I play with my fingers. Pinball machine. Replay! My coat sleeve is dirty and worn out like I am a bum. There is everything on there—bone marrow, valve oil from a trumpet, cigarette burn holes, mayonnaise, coffee. I have gotten to be a mess. Like a flashlight dimming out in the dark. Watching. One points to the other, the other points back. Stab! Stab! Two boys standing on a pile of meat doing it to each other. Doing it. Fingers. They fall down. Go up the sleeves. Gone. No, there's a fingernail. The tip of the finger. The fingerprint. Each one is different, they say.

Music comes on. It's the radio. I get dressed, eat some cereal. But, I'm still awake. That fucking boy. God, the water was black...black and shiny. Wrapper over a bowl of something in the refrigerator that smells for miles, all the way in the bathroom. I had a boy like that, and he got porked by another cop...porked and cut up and shot to pieces. Then, his mother said, "You fucking cops!" And, so on. So, I moved into a place like a sandwich, so I would never have the feeling of starving. And, I don't. Ever have that feeling. I don't need to get up, but I let the music play. Made my report. "Go home, Roseburg. Eat, sleep—go on nights." Play with my hands, do it to the music. Dancing boys with knives. I have chewed my way into a sandwich, and I'll never be hungry, again. A dirty sandwich with music and a green light. Shit in the refrigerator, dead bulbs everywhere.

What does the green and blue—no, red and blue—sign say? It says, "Heaven & Stark!" What does that mean up on the bridge in big lights? All night, all day. Maybe it says something else. The light in here: it's changed, it's like margarine. Some of the bulbs are burned out. Reflected on the water. I can't remember. Men in the sign, on a scaffold: "Got the gun!" I am on the deck, wet hair on my shoe. "Okay!" one guy starts to cough, but I know he is trying to keep from throwing up. Now I don't remember what the sign said.

I am wearing a gun; coat buttoned to the chin; shoes wet and tied tight. If I fall asleep like this I will wake up sick and bruised. I am never going to fall asleep. My eyes are like warm asphalt. My dick has shrunk down to a cold little potato, nuts crawled up inside me, warming themselves against my intestines. I was wearing gloves. Where are my gloves? In the bag? They were a mess. Seventeen dollars. But, I should've thrown them in the water or the rubbish, not in the bag. Now, they will think they were his. Nah, they won't think anything. His mother and father will get the gloves. So what. They won't recognize them; it will give them something to wonder about. "Where did these gloves come from?" They will think. And, they will get cleaned and given away, or thrown out. If I don't fall asleep, I won't wake up, so I will be fine. My shoes will dry out, the radio will play. I will never fuck or jack off, again, and I will eat air. I live in a cafeteria: "Misery? Gravy? Guts? A fight between brothers? With or without cream?"

You know I am just feeling sorry for myself. I am in the dregs. Go for a walk. I live on a nice street. All families. People are happy to have me around...in case something happens. But, no-one invites me in their house.

Walk back to the bridge. That fucking boy. I hate psychology. "Sit on it, punk." In the daytime it is so sad and busy. I am walking out there. There is a sidewalk. I can't tell if I am doing this in my mind, or if I am really walking. I'm hot. My eyes hurt. There's a workman with a hose. The cars are all covered with soot and dust. Stomach. My stomach is emptied for cleaning. Little colored rocks and plastic mermaids. The blue and white sign is off. Blue and red. Red and blue. One finger pokes another. They are up there changing the bulbs. The music from the radio in my left fingers. I am crushing it. Ha, ha! I can hear all the pieces falling on the concrete. Flutes and violins, a broken piano. I have fallen asleep. The gun hurts and I am holding it. Is this a re-enactment? "Don't move, I am a cop!" Nobody moves. There's nobody there. It's a steel girder. No, it's a man. Very stiff. I go up a tiny ladder. The city is white...completely white. There is nothing to see. It is a throat gulping air, smoke. A poison frog, its lips turning backward on itself like a sleeve, up over its eyes...the empty stomach pops out...the heart, everything. It is an asshole. I am dreaming. It is the back of my head.

My fingers have a crappy conversation going...dirtier and dirtier...whenever I stop and look at them they are going at it: poke, poke! Tilt! Fuck you! They accuse and kill each other. They go up my sleeves. They start over. Nothing gets settled. The sun is green, the scaffolding is wet. There are little paint drops everywhere, like different colored stars. A wild shot. Then, one at my own body. Nothing hurts, I swear. That one went right through the palm of the other hand. Poke, poke! Ha, ha! They just don't know how to talk to each other, do they? Got a scissor-hold on the wet steel. Yellow and red squeezing out through a hole in my jacket. Ugly, wormlike and gasping. Had a boy like that. Fucker. Shoot him in the potato. It's like it's been in the freezer. My lips kissing the metal, paint coming off in my teeth. It's covered with frost, but it manages to bleed, music far below. A boat, or is it a truck? Shoot those fuckers back out of there—those little weasels hiding up in there. BOOM! BOOM! Right through the cloth. Everything falls out, it seems. Goes down my pants. I am so hungry now. Oh, I am hungry, really. There's no blood in my feet, and my forehead is cold. I'm asleep. I'm puking on the carpet, falling off the sofa into the puke. It's too big. It stinks. It's all one planet. I don't need an excuse. Fuck off.

1990

In the California Sun

They washed the windows every six months just to get themselves wet. The rest of the year the dust stuck to their sweaty shirts and faces. Thin yellow clay dribbled down their foreheads, into their eyes. They dabbed at their faces with sticky handkerchiefs.

"What do you think, Bob?"

"Do it over."

"Okay."

Phil got down off the ladder, picked up the hose and sprayed the window. The sun poured down like heavy lemon sauce.

The two men operated a gas station in the Mojave desert. No town, nothing. There was a little house next to the gas station. Bob lived in the house. Phil slept on a steel cot in a storage room behind the garage. Bob was the mayor, Phil was the citizen. Apparently, Phil re-elected Bob every year, because Bob went on living in the house, and Phil stayed in the garage. The idiot nature of things.

"Hey, Bob, there's a car."

Both men looked down the long, straight highway.

"Yes, that's a car, alright."

"Maybe it's a woman."

"Maybe."

At first the car looked black like an ant, crawling along the shimmering asphalt, but when it got closer, it turned out to be a bloody maroon. The men watched the car with burning eyes; it was moving pretty fast—100, 110. It screamed past the station, then skidded to a stop a quarter of a mile up the road, raising a big cloud of yellow dust. The car backed up, weaving all over the highway, and came to a stop, finally, by the pumps. The windows were down. It was a woman.

"Who's in charge, here?" She had a man's voice, and two days growth.

"Are you a man or a woman?"

"I need to cash a check. I need some cash."

"You goddamn queer, this isn't a bank, it's a gas station. If you want some gas, fine, otherwise get the fuck out of here. And we don't take no cards, no checks, nothing. If you're out of cash you're out of luck."

"Aw, Bob, you are a rude, unfriendly sonofabitch, you know that?" Then, stooping so he could look right into the queen's face, he said, "You're not bad looking. Mmm-hmm. But you need a shave, honey. Now, what can I do for you? Check under the hood?" He was already around the front of the car undoing the latch.

"No, all I want...."

The hood sprang open and Phil leaned down into the smoldering engine.

"All I want is....

"I can't hear you." He was yanking wires out right and left, dislodging hoses. "Okay, start her up...."

THE NOON NEWS

This is the morning I went to get interviewed by Susan Hutchison on the *Noon News* (KIRO), having been selected "Best Poet" of 1989, by readers of the *Seattle Weekly*.

I woke up late. There was just time to shave and dress. My left hand was paralyzed and twisted into the shape of a turkey. The pain was nauseating, my vision pressed into two black ovals. Trying to move my fingers I broke into a sweat and almost threw up on the bed. It is something that happens from time to time—A charley horse? Some little bones out of place?—but, I was in a hurry and didn't have time to just lay there with my eyes closed and wait for the pain to go away. Fortunately, my refrigerator had not been defrosted for a long time. There was a heavy cake of ice in the freezer. I got out of bed, and with my right hand opened the refrigerator door. Then, I carefully lifted my left hand and laid it in the freezer, as though it was a delicate fish. Indeed, the thing looked completely dead, although it continued to generate terrible shocks of pain that seemed to go straight to my stomach.

"A beige shirt and a brown tie," I thought, as my hand turned blue on its bed of poison ice. "A vest of some sort. I'm going to be a *nice* poet, today." When my hand was throbbing from being frozen —which was much more bearable than the other pain—I went to the closet and got some pants and the beige shirt. I pulled on the pants and started to get into the shirt. "*Whaaaaa!*" My hand and wrist had thawed. I couldn't move my arm, couldn't get at the left sleeve. The pants were down around my knees. I crawled back to the refrigerator and stuck my whole forearm in the freezer. "If I can just get my pants buttoned and get my arm into this shirt, I can go sit on the toilet." Sometimes the quiet distraction of taking a crap helped me to forget about the blinding pain in my hand. When the thing was good and frozen, I got up off the floor and, operating like a man under torture—"Do what you have to do"—I got half dressed and walked stoically to the bathroom, carrying a bundle of restaurant napkins, cigarettes and a book. Once again, for no reason I can understand, the old formula worked. *"Ahhhh. Ohhhh. It's gone!"* I flexed my fingers and wiped with my revived left hand. Then, I got up, buttoned my shirt and pants, and washed my face, wiping my eyes and cheeks on my sleeve.

In my room I put on a brown tie and a brown vest. Then I got my shaving gear and went back to the bathroom. The terrible hand thing had taken a lot of time, and I had to hurry. The bus where I live only runs once an hour. I shaved with dangerous abandon, the shaver going like a lunatic fighter plane. No cuts. I tightened the tie and looked in the mirror. "Now, there's a nice guy. The type of poet you'd like to bring home...and slap around a little, smear some shit on his face." My hair was combed like Napoleon Bonaparte.

I made the bus. Downtown, I had all sorts of time to kill. I walked around on Fourth Avenue thinking about what I was going to say on television. Plug my book. Thank people. Change the subject to the Khmer Rouge and Cambodia, Israel....Uhhhh. No, be very smooth and ingratiating, with a hint of something mad and unpredictable under the surface. Hijack the newsroom. My thoughts twirled and fluttered. Finally, I lost interest in the interview, and just walked, looking at the big flat buildings and the zippy little people. I was hungry. I wanted coffee. The idea of *the poet* going on TV made me wretched and nervous. I felt like a fake, a spy.

On the sidewalk in front of one of the big, busy buildings lay a woman, good and pregnant, who had given up on panhandling. She was just laying there, trying to sleep, kind of submerged in the ocean of commerce; wingtips and high heels, Italian shoes and white-white jogging shoes whisking past her half closed eyes like fish—each one on a desperate mission. I felt like an idiot in my poet costume, without enough money to really do her any good. And, what could I say to her? "Don't drink when you're pregnant?" She didn't look like a drinker, she looked like someone who had just been dropped out of the sky, who found herself drowning in inhospitality, thoughtless cruelty—which is the most frightening kind of cruelty.

I gave the pregnant woman most of my money, and my doctor's telephone number. My doctor wouldn't charge her anything, and might give her some good leads. I asked her if she was a drinker, and she said she was not. I couldn't think of anything else smart to say, so I just drifted back into the sea of shoes.

Ha, ha, ha! The dandied up poet helps the pregnant woman and goes on television! Maybe I should talk about this woman? Sick of walking back and forth, I went into a restaurant and bought a cup of coffee.

I sat with my coffee, a kind of foolish mutt mistakenly entered in a dog show—tongue out, eager, not much going on upstairs—surrounded by clean, posturing, intelligent looking animals. The effect of the necktie and perfect shave had worn off. Anyway, I have always had shaving bumps. Across from me, two men I guessed to be in their late fifties sat eating breakfast. I watched them eat: one fork-full of egg, a nibble of carefully buttered toast, a neat sip of coffee. Dab the lips with a napkin. One of the men wore an expensive wool overcoat. I looked down at my cup and thought about becoming a pathologist—that is my new plan. I got a refill.

After the refill, I had to go to the toilet. I walked down a narrow, undecorated hallway to the men's room. The man in the wool overcoat was right behind me in the hall. I held the door open for him and he followed me into the men's room. Though there was another urinal and the shitter was empty, he stopped a few feet from my back, and just stood there.

"I was in the war," he said.

"Oh." What war? WW II? Korea? Viet Nam? Why tell me, now, while I've got my dick out and I'm trying to piss?

"I'm going to shoot you, fucker."

I turned around just a little and saw that he had his hand in his pocket; he was staring at my back—through it—between the shoulder blades. I looked at the wall in front of me. No graffiti, nothing. Shiny pipes, shiny paint.

"What war?" I asked, in a restrained, but slightly sing-songy voice.

"Korea. I'm going to shoot you, fucker."

I just kept pissing, thinking about the woman on the sidewalk, the television.

"What year?"

"Fifty-one, fifty-two."

"Very hot."

"I'm going to shoot you."

I finished, shook it, zipped, turned in some way that I imagined looked casual—and maybe did—and said,

"Excuse me."

I walked past the man, opened the door, walked down the hall straight to the front door of the restaurant, and left. It was a cafeteria—I had already paid.

Whaaaa! Oooooo! That was inside. I looked at my watch and walked to the bus stop. My stomach was riddled with little sores—coffee, fear, shame, trepidation. "Got to tell all this on the news show," I thought. "The pregnant woman, my hand, killer in the men's room. This *is* a poem. They will understand why I am a poet, when I tell them how hard it is for me to get from one place to another." My bus pulled up to the curb, and I got on, twitching and frogging. My legs were too long. I felt dizzy. "Throw up down the back of that woman's dress....No, no." My lips fused together, mouth vanished, skin turned the color of frozen turkey. "A color pathologists get familiar with," I thought.

At the TV station I sat on the steps outside, meditating, smoking, fiddling with my hair and necktie.

"You can't sit here on these steps." The security guard had come out.

"I'm on the *Noon News.*"

The man got my name and went into the building. After awhile he came back outside and said I could keep sitting there. But, my presence was an anomaly—like the mutt feeling in the restaurant. Everyone going in and out of the TV station seemed to glisten; all blindingly well-dressed, groomed and made up. And, for them it was effortless—a condition and posture they assumed without thought.

In the lobby, a woman assembled the people who were going to be on the news: a rescue worker from the earthquake, an author who wrote a book about Marilyn Monroe, some other people, and me, the poet. She led us into the glamorous and bustling news room, and sat us on some little folding chairs against a wall. I tried to make conversation with the author. He was wearing about two pounds of gold. Bracelets, watch, rings, necklace—gold everywhere.

"It's just another book about Marilyn Monroe...a piece of crap," he said. But, that's not what he said on TV.

Just before every ad they said all the headlines: "Blah, blah, blah...blah, blah, blah, and a poet." It sounded very funny. During one of the ads a big rather gruesome looking man took me by the arm. "Let's go," he said, like a jail guard moving me from one cell to another. Polite, but very definite. He sat me down in a chair and clipped a microphone on my shirt.

Susan Hutchison, who is the anchor on that show, sat next to me. Although her appearance was in every way manufactured to suit the dustless and unearthly environment of the KIRO newsroom—she seemed literally sculpted into it—I recognized her, suddenly, as human. A shock amid all the folderol—the teleprompters, ice blue furnishings, the chattering news machines. I think she was not sure what to do with me. She hoped I had brought a poem to read, but I hadn't. I explained that my poems were all too long, and none of them were suitable for broadcast on commercial television. Then, the ad was over.

We had a pleasant and ordinary conversation about writing and performing poetry. I got it across that being a poet is a job like any other. Like being a news anchor, for instance. Susan Hutchison is an intelligent and fairly spontaneous person literally stuffed into a flawless and uncompromising monstrosity.

I did not plug my book or mention my crippled hand. Nor did I talk about the pregnant woman on the sidewalk. Or, the Korean War veteran who maybe almost shot me in the bathroom. I did not say one word about where poetry comes from. Nothing, not a word.

When the interview was over I left the TV station, got on a bus and went home, back to my room. I took off my tie and tried to start the day over, as though everything that had happened so far was a loop that could be snipped off, as though it was fiction.

1989